P9-DOF-651

my one hundred adventures

my one hundred adventures

polly horvath

schwartz & wade books • new york

Published by Schwartz & Wade Books
an imprint of Random House Children's Books
a division of Random House, Inc.
New York

Visit us on the Web! www.randomhouse.com/kids
Educators and librarians, for a variety of teaching tools,
visit us at www.randomhouse.com/teachers

Library of Congress Cataloging-in-Publication Data
Horvath, Polly.
My one hundred adventures / Polly Horvath.—1st ed.
p. cm.
Summary: Twelve-year-old Jane, who lives at the beach in a run-down old
house with her mother, two brothers, and sister, has an eventful summer
accompanying her pastor on bible deliveries, meeting former boyfriends of her
mother's, and being coerced into babysitting for a family of ill-mannered
children, all the while learning valuable lessons about life.
ISBN 978-0-375-84582-6 (trade) — ISBN 978-0-375-95582-2 (glb)
[1. Brothers and sisters—Fiction. 2. Single-parent families—Fiction.
3. Summer—Fiction. 4 Beaches—Fiction. 5. Babysitters—Fiction.] I. Title.
PZ7.H79224My 2008
[Fic]—dc22
2008002243

The text of this book is set in Weiss.
Book design by Rachael Cole
Printed in the United States of America

10 9 8 7 6 5 4 3 2 1

First Edition

To Arnie,
Emily Willa
and
Rebecca Avery

And with enormous gratitude to
Anne Schwartz, Amy Berkower
and Jack Gantos

contents

Summer Begins

All summers take me back to the sea. There in the long eelgrass, like birds' eggs waiting to be hatched, my brothers and sister and I sit, grasses higher than our heads, arms and legs like thicker versions of the grass waving in the wind, looking up at the blue washed sky. My mother is gathering food for dinner: clams and mussels and the sharply salty greens that grow by the shore. It is warm enough to lie here in the little silty puddles like bathwater left in the tub after the plug has been pulled. It is the beginning of July and we have two months to live out the long, nurturing days, watching the geese and the saltwater swans and the tides as they are today, slipping out, out, out as the moon pulls the other three seasons far away wherever it takes things. Out past the planets, far away from Uranus and the edge of our solar system, into the brilliantly lit dark where the things we don't know about yet reside. Out past my childhood, out past the ghosts, out past the breakwater of the stars. Like the silvery lace curtains of my bedroom being drawn from my window, letting in light, so the moon gently pulls back the layers of the year, leaving the best part open and free. So summer comes to me.

"Jane, Maya, Hershel, Max," calls my mother. She always calls my name first. She is finished gathering and her baskets are heavy. We run to help her bring things back to the house. No one else lives year-round on the beach but us. A poet with no money can still live very well, my mother reminds us, and I do not know why. Who would think having to leave the ocean for most of the year is a better way to live? How could we not live well, the five of us together? I love our house. I love the bedroom I share with my sister. Our house has no upstairs like the houses of my friends. It has one floor with a kitchen that is part of a larger room, and off of this large room with its big table and rocking chairs and its soft old couch and armchair and miles of booklined shelves are three bedrooms. One for my mother, one for my brothers, one for my sister and me. "I love this house," I say to my mother often. "You cannot love it as I do," she says. "No one can ever love it as I do."

There's a big red-and-white-checked oilcloth on the kitchen table and an old wine bottle with a dripping candle in the center of it. Our bedroom has two sagging cots topped with old Pendleton blankets. My mother says there is nothing like a Pendleton blanket for keeping you warm at night. She says this especially on nights when the storms are coming in from the northeast and the house is cold and the wind is blowing through the cracks and we read books by candlelight because the electricity is out again. We love the winter because when our power goes out there are no other houses alight on this shore. Their occupants have all gone home until next summer. We are all alone. It is darker than dark then. You can hear the waves crash louder when it is dark. You can smell the sharper smells of the sea. Maybe the wind will take us this time, I think, as a gust shakes the foundations of the house. Maybe we will be blown apart to the many corners of the earth, and I am filled with sadness to lose the other four, but then a sharp stab of something, excitement maybe. It is the prospect of adventures to be had.

On Sundays we walk as we always do, fall, winter, spring, summer, any weather, to the little steepled church in town. We get sand in our good church shoes walking over the beach and sit on cement dividers when we get to the parking lot, dumping our shoes, as much a church ritual now as kneeling at prayer. The church is just the right size, not too large. It has two rooms, one of which is for the Sunday schoolers. We stand in the woody-smelling pews with the soft, much-opened hymnbooks and sing. But despite all this churchgoing every Sunday of every year, it isn't until this year, when I am twelve, that I have figured out I can pray. Perhaps I have had nothing to pray for until now. As if itchy and outgrown, my soul is twisting about my body, wanting something more to do this summer than the usual wading in the shallows and reading and building castles on the shore. I want something I know not what, which is what adventures are about. The step into the know-not-what. I want it so badly it is making me bad-tempered with Maya, who is too young to understand. She wants every summer the same, and so had I until this year. And my brothers are too young to care about anything like this for a long time. I am twisting all alone.

This week our preacher, a fat old lady named Nellie Phipps, says from her pulpit that you ought to pray all the time. Just about anything at all. It doesn't have to be sacred. And your prayers will be answered, she declares, your prayers will always be answered.

I pray for a hundred adventures. And maybe, I think, if I pray all the time unceasingly as Nellie is telling us we should, as I walk to town and help my mother shuck oysters, as I make baskets from reeds and sweep the floors or weed the vegetable garden, as I sit mooning over the movement of the wind and lying on my back, lost in the thoughtlessness of doing nothing, then there might be a response. And so I do and maybe it is because of this that it all happens.

Who would think that the universe would pay any attention to me? Who would think that someone who looks like Nellie Phipps would know?

A Stranger Comes
My First Adventure

....

The Strawberries Are Ripe

It is at the end of a long summer day. My brothers are freckled with the sun and Maya and I have sunburned shoulders. And everyone's hair is dry and sticky with the sea. We have sand in our swimsuits and hang around outside by the picnic table as my mother goes in and out of the house, making salads and stirring the sun tea.

"Mayas were Indians," I say to Maya because she has come across her name in a book. Or thinks she has.

"Where did they live?" she asks.

"I don't know. Mexico, I think," I say. "And they had strange-looking round clay calendars. Our teacher had one she brought back from a trip to

Mexico, only not a real one. She hung it in the classroom. I don't remember anything else about the Mayas except they had gold." And then I think maybe that is the Aztecs but I don't bother to tell Maya this. I like being able to answer her questions even if I am wrong.

"I would like to have gold," says Maya. "I would make jewelry out of it."

"I think the Mayas did too," I say. "We can go to the library tomorrow and look it up."

The library in summer is the most wonderful thing because there you get books on any subject and read them each for only as long as they hold your interest, abandoning any that don't, halfway or a quarter of the way through if you like, and store up all that knowledge in the happy corners of your mind for your own self and not to show off how much you know or spit it back at your teacher on a test paper.

Mrs. Spinnaker comes out from next door. She is the only one on the beach like us without a lot of money. She has no sailboat or fancy things. She comes every year with her little black terrier, Horace, who runs to our picnic table when we are there and barks us into submission. "HORACE, you leave those children alone," she says, and stalks grumpily over, scooping him up, never acknowledging us, irritated because we have given Horace a chance to misbehave and make her wrong.

"But we don't mind, Mrs. Spinnaker," we tell her. We like Horace the way you like a familiar annoyance that spells home. He is part of our summers like the oysters and the sun tea and the sandy bare feet around the table. We wonder if Mrs. Spinnaker knows our names the way we know hers and Horace's. Does she hear our mother call us? Does she sit by her little cottage window and eavesdrop? Does she know not just our names but our characters? That Maya is afraid of things? That my mother rises in the night to write poetry? That Hershel doesn't eat the peas, as the rest of us do, right off the vine, and that Max is always seeing whales? "It's another whale," he cries, and we all nod and smile. Who knows? Maybe he does see them. Maybe there are whales the rest of us cannot see. Does Mrs. Spinnaker put her head out the side window, the window not visible from our house, so that we cannot see her looking out to sea, checking for Max's whales?

Don't worry, Mrs. Spinnaker, I want to yell to her, in case she does this and it troubles her—it's always okay to do things just in case. It's better to be fooled a hundred times than never to look. Who cares if you are fooled? And I make my one hundredth prayer.

Maybe it is a coincidence. Or maybe we never know why our prayers are answered. But anyhow, we are sitting down to dinner and I have prayed my one hundredth prayer when he shows up.

He is a tall man with shaggy hair and bad teeth, in a suit too big for his sharp, elbowy frame. He looks like a clothes hanger. I keep staring at him thinking he is the wrong shape for his suit. That he looks old, although you can tell he isn't really, and the suit looks worn and what is he doing at our picnic table?

My mother must think he looks hungry because she invites him to sit down and eat and he does without any more preamble than that. He fills his plate with my mother's good food, the oysters and the corn bread and the salad made from the greens in our garden and the greens from the sea and says how good it all is and I think maybe he is thin because he is always hungry. And when he is done he rises, we have hardly begun our own dinners—hunger has given him an efficient way to eat—and he says, "I'd like to thank you all by taking you to a fair."

"No reason to thank us," says my mother. "You were welcome to it. You were invited."

"Not many people would have invited me," he says.

"Well, I don't know about that," says my mother. "Not Mrs. Spinnaker, perhaps," and she laughs. Then she covers her mouth with her hands as if the laugh surprises her. I think it amazes her that this man has pulled such candor out of her. "Anyhow, stay a bit if you like. Have some dessert. Our strawberries are ripe."

"Ummm," says the man. "I'd like to do that."

He settles back down into one of our Adirondack chairs by the side of the house and waits politely for all of us to finish eating. We are made self-conscious by an audience that isn't Mrs. Spinnaker.

My mother picks a big bowl of strawberries and

brings out the sugar bowl and some milk to put on them. There aren't quite enough to go around, and my brothers look worried that this stranger is going to get theirs, so I eat only one and say I am full. I wonder what to do at the table, until Max stands up and says he sees a whale, and that gives me an excuse to walk down to the ocean for a better look.

When I get back we are going to the fair after all.

It doesn't take long to wash up. My mother makes us grab sweaters. Evenings grow cool when the sun goes down, she warns. Then adds, If we stay that long at the fair, as if she has been presumptuous.

"I didn't even know there was a fair in town," she says to the man as we walk along. "There hasn't been much commotion about it. No flyers or signs. I haven't heard people talking of it. Not even the children at church. Usually our minister will warn of such things. 'Children, don't go run and join the circus!' That sort of caution."

"Well, I don't believe children do that very often, if they ever did," says the man. He has a slow, lanky stride and a slow, lanky way of piecing his words together to go with it, a kind of disheveled looseness that is very calming. As if he knows holding it all together isn't very important. It does not calm my mother, though; she is under some great restrained excitement that would make the air buzz if she let any of it escape. As if she is full of little bubbles, which if she opens her mouth too much will carbonate the air all around us. I watch her carefully, expecting her to float off into the sky, carried away on the corked gaseous wonder of the evening.

"It must be a very small fair," she decides.

"It is. It is a very small fair," says the man, and that is all. We walk in silence.

When we get there we see he is right. They have set up on the park by the public beach where we seldom go, having a beach of our own. There are a Ferris wheel and a merry-go-round and something called the Octopus. None of us has ever been on rides before and I guess we wouldn't now except the man knows some of the men who run them. We don't ask how. They let us on for free.

We ride and get off and ride again. I wish he knew the men at the cotton candy stall. There is only one food stall but it sells most everything you could possibly want, cotton candy and candy apples, hot dogs and snow cones and caramel corn. I turn my head and try not to smell and try especially not to look, to betray any desire. My brothers are so busy riding, their heads in such a spin that they have no time for such thoughts, and it turns out Maya likes the rides fine but her stomach doesn't. I have to keep taking her off behind a tent where the Porta Potties are. She thinks she is going to be sick but never is.

The air goes round and round, pushed by the wind of the whirling rides, and children crying out in delight move every which way. The park is in a swirl. We are all rushing about, and I think how nobody smashes into anyone else although all is movement. We make eddies and channels in the air with our bodies between the rides and the movement of the rides and the movement of our breath, and all the time the ocean slaps into shore back and forth, back and forth, its eternal movement seeming suddenly prosaic in comparison to this froth we create on the shore. And I realize we are all more powerful than the sea, able to go as we wish, unlike the steady coming and going of the tide, which is powerless to change its prescribed motion.

My mother lets us stay after the sun has set. She and the man keep walking around. At one point we see them down on the public dock, just sitting, talking and watching the stars come out. Another time she is settled back against the side of a shed and he has one hand resting over her head, sort of leaning over her as he talks, and she has one foot off the ground, playing with a shoe in a way I have never seen her do before.

On one of Maya's trips to the Porta Potti we see them laughing and joking around with one of the men who run the Octopus. They get on and ride around and around and the man running the ride doesn't make them get off in between the way he does everyone else.

"Does Mama like that man?" asks Maya.

"I don't see how she can, she just met him," I say.

"I guess you can like someone you've just met," says Maya. "I do sometimes."

"Well, I guess you can," I say, "but it sure doesn't seem like Mama."

I am hungry and tired and it is time to go home. Even the boys are tired. Every star in the universe is out and it is so bright about us it almost makes us trip over our feet, blinded by ambient light, distracted by sparkles.

The man doesn't walk back to our house with us but stops by an old car parked on Main Street.

"This is mine," he says. "I guess I'll be going now."

"Well, well," says my mother, meaning nothing by it, I can tell. Just making a sound.

"Thanks for dinner," says the man.

"Thanks for the fair," says my mother.

Once he drives off we make our way back to our house through the thickness of the night. My mother makes toast that she and I eat, sitting at the kitchen table, staring in the direction of the rushing sound of the invisible sea, which keeps us company always here so that none of us is ever really alone.

My brothers and sisters are in bed, exhausted and sandy. My mother didn't even make them wash first but I suppose after such an adventure it doesn't matter. My mother does not usually have adventures either and she seems all dreamy with the memory of this one. She sits and her shoe hangs off one foot the way it did with the man and she plays with it and looks out the window again as if her past is contained there in the movement of the invisible sea. We eat more toast.

"I'm off to bed now," I say. "I wonder if we'll see that man again tomorrow."

"I don't expect we will. It isn't like him to come around more than once a century or so," she says, and smiles to herself.

As I go to bed I think what an odd thing to say about someone you don't even know. But then, he does come. He comes again in the morning and brings a bouquet of daisies and leaves it at our door with a note that says he is off now for good. And as he walks away my mother hums a little tune to herself.

"That was your father," she says, and hangs the laundry on the line, shooing away the boys, who are stirring up dust around the clean, wet clothes.

Mrs. Parks's Thrombosis

My Second Adventure

Later in the day I look at Max and Maya and Hershel. Does any of us look like the clothes hanger man? It doesn't feel possible to me that my brothers or sister or I could have a father. And we are all so different. Max is small and dark and Hershel and I have sandy hair. Maya is round and rosy and light. It doesn't seem to me that such a person as the clothes hanger man could have fathered us. If it were important, wouldn't my mother have mentioned it before now?

Perhaps my mother was having a poet's flight of fancy. She is always finding things on the shore or in the lagoon and bringing them into the house to dry, rocks and shells and starfish. She sometimes

brings things home from the sea that we don't rec-
ognize. Odd bits of sponge and sea life. Then she
names them. And in that moment we all believe
her. It is mermaid hair, seahorse halter, Persephone
weed, your father.

This is always how I thought she found us.
Washed up on shore. Carrying us home in her
pockets. Jane, Maya, Max, Hershel. That she is
enough in herself alone to have made us. That she
has dreamt us into being.

And now I think she has found this man and
decided to give us a father to view. She has found
him on the rocks, aired him out, brought him
into our house, and will later return him to the sea.
This feels right to me and I return him happily
there myself. I don't need this father, I want to
say to her. I am happy with things as they are.
You don't have to scrounge one from the sea to
satisfy me.

I am thinking these thoughts and staring out the
window when I see a woman making her way
across the beach to our house. It is Mrs. Merriweather from the church. Finally she reaches our
door and knocks on it and my mother answers.
Mrs. Merriweather has news! She doesn't know

my mother very well but they both know Mrs. Parks. Mrs. Parks has had a thrombosis!

"My heavens, when did this occur?" asks my mother, always concerned for the sick and dying. She writes them poems when there is nothing else to be done.

"Nobody knows exactly when it *occurred*," says Mrs. Merriweather. She is eyeing the big plate of just-made oatmeal cookies on our kitchen table. She sits down and eats three rapidly as if afraid that at any moment we will tell her to stop.

When she speaks again it is with a full mouth. "But she *noticed* it early this morning when she was out with her geese."

"Those geese would cause anyone to thrombose," says my mother, sitting down and eating a cookie herself.

"They are evil birds. All birds are evil as far as I'm concerned, but geese are the most evil. Bad intentions bespeak bad hearts, and geese come at you and bite. Well, anyway, I would be happy to stay with Mrs. Parks—she's taken a notion that the thing may travel up to her brain and snap out her lights like this!" Mrs. Merriweather snaps her fingers to demonstrate.

"My, my," says my mother. She has laundry on the line, and a look at the sky tells us it might have to be taken down anytime soon, but you don't leave a neighbor to have her lights snapped out by a wandering thrombosis over a trifle like clean clothes.

"I would normally be happy to stay with her and keep watch for any unusual brain activity, but you know it's strawberry season and I've promised to drive up to Maine today with some for my sister Beatrice."

"Is she jamming?" asks my mother. "I am making strawberry jam myself this week."

"It isn't just *that*, my dear. I wouldn't leave Mrs. Parks for *that*. No, it's that I promised her berries. Their strawberries are no good up there. It's a queer dark tree-laden state. Full of old lumberjacks and bears and those dark, tart blueberries. Not like here, where our sweet little strawberries grow."

"All they have are bitter berries," agrees my mother.

Mrs. Merriweather nods, thankful that my mother understands. They are fast becoming friends. "No . . . flavor . . . a-tall," whispers Mrs. Merriweather as if to seal their friendship with a conspiracy. "Now, I don't like to be a fussbudget but even if I took the day shift with Mrs. Parks and drove up tonight like the very devil, I'm afraid those berries when I got them to her would be *mush*. They're already picked at their peak. You know berries. But, of course, if this is not convenient for you, what with the children . . ."

"The children can come with me. Or Jane can watch them here. But I think they should come. They might cheer up Mrs. Parks. Perhaps they could take turns reading to her. Or rub her feet."

Maya and Max and Hershel look a bit wild-eyed at that. We are hovering in the background, waiting for the upshot of this visit.

"I'll come back for the night shift, then, dearie. I will be late but I will be here," says Mrs. Merriweather.

"I'm sure you're one hundred percent reliable," says my mother, and shakes Mrs. Merriweather's hand, which seems at once an oddly formal and a too intimate gesture. She is overcome by emotion at the thought of Mrs. Merriweather's goodness. Of her own.

"Summer storms are so fierce," says my mother as she finds her purse. Mrs. Merriweather nods. I know my mother is thinking of the laundry again and whether or not to take it off the line before we go. Mrs. Merriweather does not know why my mother is talking about storms. Mrs. Merriweather nods and smiles all the same. My mother is doing her a great favor.

"I don't want our underwear carried out to sea," my mother goes on.

"Well, no, of *course* you wouldn't. Of *course* you wouldn't want *that*," says Mrs. Merriweather, hustling us all out the door. She is passionately agreeable in her hurry to get us to Mrs. Parks's.

"No, let's leave the laundry where it is," says my mother as we start across the beach for the parking lot and Mrs. Merriweather's car. It is always a treat to get a car ride. "Let's be optimists."

"I like your attitude," says Mrs. Merriweather, huffing and puffing as her feet sink, leaving deep prints in the sand.

Mrs. Parks's house is a grim, old, narrow, gray thing, as parched and slit-eyed and suspicious-looking as Mrs. Parks. I do not know Mrs. Parks well, only from church and the looks she gives me or Maya or my brothers if we wiggle too much during the service.

My mother has brought a basket of her good lettuce for Mrs. Parks. When she opens the door, I can see that she needs stronger measures of hope than even my mother's lettuce can provide.

"I'M DYING!" Mrs. Parks cries. She grabs my mother around the neck and propels her down the steps.

"Oh no!" says my mother, who has not anticipated being sucked into such a climactic occurrence quite so early in the visit. "Oh no."

"It's only a matter of time before THE THROM-BOSIS REACHES MY BRAIN!"

"Mrs. PARKS!" shouts my mother. "Why has Dr. Callahan not put you in the hospital? Oh my lord, what is he *doing*? He mustn't let you die like this!"

It turns out this is Mrs. Parks's way of thinking as well. She explains that Dr. Callahan has not put her in the hospital because her illness is too boring.

"Well, it isn't boring for *you*," says my mother in her most supportive manner.

"They're all the same, these doctors. They want young patients with interesting illnesses. People whom it makes sense to save. Suppose he saves me? So what? It won't be long before I just up and die of something else, that's the way *he* looks at it. I'm eighty years old. When you're eighty they whisper, Well, if you won't tell anyone you're thrombosing, Mrs. Parks, I won't either."

"Oh no. To say such a thing to you!" declares my mother.

"Or something like that," says Mrs. Parks, looking shifty-eyed. "He told me Mrs. Nasters has cancer, but he sent *her* to the hospital because she's got an *interesting* illness. They can all stand around and *stare* at her."

"I'm sure they're not going to stare at Mrs. Nasters. She wouldn't stand for it," says my mother. "What is happening to our congregation? Both you and Mrs. Nasters struck down in the prime of life."

We all look a little startled at this statement, but especially Mrs. Parks.

I think what it will mean to have both Mrs. Nasters and Mrs. Parks missing from church on Sunday. They wear hats with fruit on them. When I get bored I stare at their fruited hats. I wonder if we can convince some of the younger old ladies to take up fruited straw hats. Like passing the torch. Or will they regard this as some kind of next-in-line-for-the-tomb designation? My mother wears a straw hat to guard against the sun but her hat is fruitless. I think sadly of her in old age, adding every year a cherry.

"He hardly talked about my thrombosis with me. He had no interest. He just wanted to gossip as usual. As if nothing much were wrong!" says Mrs. Parks.

Dr. Callahan is the only doctor in our small Massachusetts town and the clearinghouse for a lot of gossip. My mother says we don't even need a newspaper with Dr. Callahan around.

"He sent me home to die but I'm not going to do it," says Mrs. Parks.

"Good for you," says my mother.

"I'm going to go visit my sister in California in-stead."

"Well, that seems like a better plan," says my mother, putting down her basket and folding her hands. She still has Mrs. Parks draped around her neck like a barnacle.

"He doesn't think so. He says not to take an air-plane unless I want my leg to explode!"

"Oh dear," says my mother, trying to disengage herself gently from Mrs. Parks's grip. I know she is just trying to keep from being strangled but the timing is unfortunate because now it looks as if she is afraid Mrs. Parks will explode on *her.*

"So you gotta drive me," says Mrs. Parks. "We must leave right now. Who knows how long it takes to get there—all the way across the country—and how long I've got? We mustn't put it off. We must seize the day."

Mrs. Parks hustles us out the front door, locking it as she goes, and herds us to her ancient car, where she pushes the four of us children willy-nilly into the backseat with no regard for the natural pecking order. Thus I end up without a window.

My mother looks uncertain as Mrs. Parks tosses

her the keys. My mother doesn't often drive but I don't think that is wholly what is bothering her. She debates quite often the efficacy of her good deeds and I think this is what she would like to do now except that the answer seems pretty clear-cut. Here is someone dying who has told her *exactly* what my mother can do for her. How can she refuse? Even with laundry on the line? So she puts Mrs. Parks in the front passenger seat, where she can pass her gum and climbs into the driver's seat.

We drive like lightning all day, stopping now and then for food and bathroom breaks. All of us children are mesmerized by the big wide world to either side of the interstate. Mrs. Parks snoozes off and on and Hershel asks considerately from time to time, "Are you dead yet?" but she never is.

"But thank you for asking," she answers.

My mother tells Hershel to stop asking Mrs. Parks if she is dead but Mrs. Parks says it is okay. Like Mrs. Merriweather, she is bowled over by my mother's easy accommodation to her needs. As if contagious, it brings out an uncharacteristic affability in her. And I think, We affect people around us so much with our moods. A depressed person can make a room gloomy and a sweet nature can cause the lion to lie down with the lamb. I think how lucky we children are to have randomly landed a mother who inspires a spirit of goodwill. Then I crawl over Hershel to take his window seat.

Halfway across the state and halfway into the night we stop at one of the restaurants perched on overpasses crossing the interstate. They seem to look down on us with their large glassed-in eyes, beckoning us up for saltwater taffy and pecan logs. Mrs. Parks buys a bag of saltwater taffy and we amble out to the parking lot overlooking the highway while my mother uses the restroom. We are all chewing thoughtfully and looking down at the tops of cars when Mrs. Parks decides she has had enough.

"I don't like all these freeways and their big trucks," she says to my mother on her return.

My brothers spit on the backs of trucks, like huge migrating animals, rushing on below. All the lovely colors of the taffy lull me. I am sleepy. I keep staring at the bag in Mrs. Parks's hand: yellows, greens, blues, whites, pastel colors so soft they look as if they have faded in the sea. The washed colors of sea and sleep. Pajama colors. The colors of baby clothes. In my nose is the smell of my brothers' heads after they are born. Maybe this is why people making journeys buy saltwater taffy. It gives you the lovely dreamy sense that you can start all over again from the beginning.

We get in the car and start driving back the way we came, hurrying down the highway. Going through a tunnel of dark, it is as if the car is going through the birth passage, being born to morning light, bearing the gift of saltwater taffy and the soft, unbloomed hearts of my brothers and sister and the worn, hopeful hearts of my mother and Mrs. Parks and my own heart, buzzing with the excitement of the night, full of want.

"And I was getting tired of sitting. I was getting a sore bottom," Mrs. Parks explains further now that we are headed home.

"But I thought you wanted to see your sister," says my mother. Then she looks at Mrs. Parks and sighs and realizes what a useless thing she has said. Mrs. Parks wanted to see her sister and now she doesn't. It is as simple as that.

Mrs. Parks keeps rotating in her seat and offering

us the bag of saltwater taffy. We only take one or two pieces each because she has paid for it. We have all slept but my mother, who has driven most of the night.

When we pull up at Mrs. Parks's house Mrs. Merriweather is standing in the doorway looking worried. We have forgotten even to leave a note. But she is so relieved, she is not angry, and she makes us eggs and Mrs. Parks smiles all through breakfast and says she feels much better.

As we prepare to depart through the kitchen door, Mrs. Parks gives Hershel the rest of the salt-water taffy. She has decided she doesn't like it after all, she says, but I think she is just relinquishing the last of the adventure. She is done with all that. She helps Mrs. Merriweather put the dishes in the dishwasher. She doesn't think Mrs. Merriweather is doing it right. Through the open door I see Max being bitten by one of the geese and my mother kicking it in the nose. The goose's beak bleeds. I did not know that if you kicked a goose it would bleed. It is disconcerting. The geese are so mean they look as if something else should be running through their veins, something vile and milky. Not blood like my own. I shove Maya the rest of the way out the door and we join my mother, Hershel and Max.

Mrs. Parks comes to the door again to wave goodbye and asks what has happened to the goose. She is staring at its bloody beak. My mother says she doesn't know. I don't think she is trying to cover up her action. I think she is too tired to explain.

We walk home because Mrs. Merriweather is too busy keeping an eye on Mrs. Parks's thrombosis to drive us, but the thrombosis seems so long ago and beside the point that we want to tell her it is ancient history. Mrs. Parks is cranky but content now. She has not stayed around to die. She has gone to visit her sister even if she never got there. She has gone into the night and bought snacks. She has found out she can still have adventures. But Mrs. Merriweather probably wouldn't understand this. She was busy at her sister's bringing berries. She has had another sort of day and will never know ours. Suddenly I realize that everyone in the whole world is, at the end of a day, staring at a dusky horizon, owner of a day that no one else will ever know. I see all those millions of different days crowded into the one.

Max says he sees a whale even though we haven't reached the beach yet and cannot see the ocean. When we get past the parking lot, my mother carries Maya across the sand because she is too tired to walk and puts her to bed. But my mother does not go to bed immediately herself, even though she has not slept. The sun is just over the horizon and the waves are gently sparkling and she and I get the laundry off the line. "Look at this, Jane," she says to me. "The clothes are all dry. They smell like the night." She gathers them into her arms. "We didn't have a storm after all. We were spared it." And she goes back into the house to rest a bit before seeing what the new day will bring.

Delivering Bibles by Balloon
My Third Adventure

It is Sunday. Nellie Phipps exhorts the congregation to pray for the speedy recovery of Mrs. Parks. We pray for the other folks in town, and then, says Nellie, we are to pray *especially* for Mrs. Nasters and her cancer. It is exactly what Mrs. Parks complained about. Why should Mrs. Nasters be given special consideration? And so I refuse to pray for Mrs. Nasters. Mrs. Parks has put me and our family firmly on her side with her underrated illness. But Nellie's sermon is about positive energy and positive thoughts and how these things affect our lives and I begin to worry about whether such closing of my heart to Mrs. Nasters's cancer will have bad effects on my adventures.

I know Nellie believes in miracles—miraculous healings, mystical events. I would like to know if these things exist too. I pray for a sign. If such things can be, then let me see a circle of purple light against the sky.

I decide to ask Nellie about these things. I also want to ask her what she thinks about my not praying for Mrs. Nasters. If that is what she means by negative energy.

At the door of the church as Nellie is shaking hands and kissing babies I grab her proffered hand and hang on to it as to a lifeline. "I have a question, Miss Phipps," I say. "A question about energy."

"Later, Jane Fielding," she says. "I've got hands to shake."

"Please, it's pressing," I say.

"You just think it's a pressing question," says Nellie Phipps. "Now go out and enjoy your youth. Young people don't have pressing issues."

There is something wrong with me, then. I feel nothing but a kind of insistent pressing. As if there is an understanding I must move toward or into.

"Please," I say.

"Be young, Jane," she says encouragingly. She

picks up one of the lilies that decorate the church and waves it from side to side. "Be like a lily. A lily. They toil not."

She twirls it in her hand.

"Neither do they spin," growls an old lady, squeezing by. She has been in line to shake hands and I have held her up. She gives up on shaking hands and heads grumpily down the steps instead.

"Can we talk after you're done?" I ask.

"Go! Go wait in the Sunday school room if you must," Nellie says. "And *consider* the lilies. They have no pressing questions. They're very ding-dong positive."

I run up the road first to ask my mother if it is okay if I come home later. She says of course it is. Sunday dinner is always in the evening at our house, as the sun sets. As if we are feasting to mark the end of another week. I know Sunday is supposed to be the beginning of the week but my mother's Sunday tranquility makes it feel as if we are putting the week to bed, pulling the covers up under its chin, blessing what has been and closing its eyes for sleep.

My mother goes off with my sister and brothers. She has much to do. Summer Sundays she spends sweeping the sand out of the cottage and changing the sheets and picking fresh flowers to go around all the rooms. I watch their innocent backs going over the crest of the hill as if I will never see them again.

I go into the Sunday school room but get shooed out by Mrs. Henderson, who is the piano teacher in town but also teaches the younger children's Sunday-school classes. She frightens me and I am glad I no longer have to return to that room with her snapping voice and heavy piano-pedal-pounding foot.

I sit on the back steps of the church by the Sunday-school room and make daisy chains from the tiny daisies growing in the church field. Finally Nellie has blessed everyone she can find, even some men stumbling out of the tavern, confusing them more than they normally are. She can no longer put off dealing with me.

"So," she says, approaching.

I tell her my worries about deliberately not praying for Mrs. Nasters.

"It's all energy," she says finally. "It's like illness.

When people are sick, it is just their own unresolved issues affecting their energies. Do you understand what I mean?"

I nod as if I have known this all along. As if this
is perfectly natural. It does make a kind of sense.

"Then Mrs. Nasters . . ."

"Cancer is usually caused by people's unresolved
anger," says Nellie. "Mrs. Nasters has a lot of work
to do. Spiritual work."

"Mrs. Parks's thrombosis?"

"Blocked energy. Are you interested in these
things, child?"

I nod. *She* is clearly interested in them. How
can I say no without being rude? But it's not this
so much that I am interested in as *something*, that
I want to find, or see, something that I know is
there, in everything, that if I can only be good
enough, or, as she believes, positive enough, I can
get a clearer glimpse of.

"Well, I should take you on my healing sessions,
then."

I must look completely blank, because she explains to me that she uses her hands to move people's energies and unblock them.

"Of course, not everyone is receptive," she says.

I would guess not. I try to imagine telling Maya or Max or Hershel, Sit still, your energy is going to be unblocked.

"Well then, come with me. I have to deliver Bibles this afternoon and I will drop in on Mrs. McCarthy. She has asked me for a healing session. Of course, she calls it *laying on of hands* because that's what the old-timers used to call it. She's in an old folks' home outside of town. We can drop in on her and spend the rest of the day delivering the Bibles in that direction, because I haven't been out that way yet."

The missionary movement within our church sends every congregation boxes of Bibles to distribute. Every week Nellie tries to rope in anyone she can to help. But as much as people seem to like Nellie Phipps, you know what Sunday is, it's a day with a lot of potential for naps.

"I ought to ask my mother," I say, getting into Nellie's car.

"When are you people going to get you a phone out there?" she asks as we drive to the parking lot closest to our beach.

"Oh gosh, Miss Phipps, I dunno," I say. My mother has five mouths to feed.

"You run on, now. I don't want to get sand in my Sunday shoes," she says. "And tell your mother you don't know if you'll be home for dinner or not. It's time-consuming to get your energies flowing again. You stopped them when you didn't pray for Mrs. Nasters but we'll release them with this positive work."

I run over the hot sand and find my mother digging some clams for dinner. I tell her I'll be gone all day and maybe won't come home until after dinner because I am going to distribute Bibles with Nellie Phipps. At this my mother straightens up and wipes her hands on her skirt and says, "Well, how in heaven did you get yourself roped into that?"

"I don't know," I lie. Nellie Phipps wants me to explain how I need to unblock my negative energies to let the positive energies flow and that Bible delivering is one step, but I know what will fly with my mother and what won't.

"Well, if you said you would I guess you'd better, though it's a shame to waste such a lovely day."

"I know," I say. "I just got stuck."

My mother nods.

I am interested in seeing Nellie do this stuff with

her hands. This sounds miraculous to me. I just don't really want to deliver Bibles. Forcing anyone to read anything doesn't sit right with me. I run back along the beach looking out to sea, praying to be distracted by whales. If I see whales, I think, it means my energy is fine and I don't have to bother with Nellie Phipps and her Bibles, but I don't see whales. I decide that this isn't conclusive. It may just mean that God isn't into the obvious.

I get in the car and Nellie and I drive right out of town, the boxes of Bibles slamming around in the back of the station wagon, which doesn't have very good springs, and so we and the Bibles bounce along the country roads, giving new meaning to the expression "Bible thumping." I don't share this with Nellie.

We stop at the old people's home first and I trail along shyly behind Nellie. She goes right up to Mrs. McCarthy's room.

"Reverend Phipps!" says Mrs. McCarthy from her bed. She is white, her skin pale with age and illness, her hair snowy and fluffy; her sheets are white, her nightgown is white. I imagine when she dies, she just melds further into this whiteness and then disappears. There is no need to bury her. It is a very clean death.

No one pays any attention to me. They are chatting as I stand there thinking about Mrs. McCarthy's whiteness. And then, as if they have done this a thousand times, Mrs. McCarthy silently lies back on the bed and closes her eyes and Nellie moves her hands slowly and deliberately about six inches over her. She does something strange over Mrs. McCarthy's head, as if she is pulling invisible things out of it.

It takes about ten minutes and then Mrs. McCarthy sits up and smiles peacefully. "Oh my," she says. "Oh my. That was powerful! Powerful!"

"Yes," says Nellie. "I'll be seeing you next week, then."

We go silently back down the stairs. I feel oddly peaceful, as if whatever Nellie was doing has affected me too.

We get into the car without a word and drive on.

Eventually this serenity fades, like bathwater seeping out a leaky drain, and I am sad that the real world and my usual feelings return and intrude. I begin to wonder if it was all in my head

back there and I look at Nellie. She doesn't look so
coolly serene anymore either. What happened and
why didn't it last? I am too shy to ask and I'm not
sure Nellie knows anyway.

We are far out of town now. Nellie says we have
to drive a long way to be in a Bible-dropping territory she hasn't covered yet. I see long wild lupins
and some kind of yellow wildflower I can't identify
and lots of fields of cows. I wish I had a flower
book with me to give these yellow flowers a name.
I ask Nellie if she knows what they are. She has
her hands gripped on the steering wheel and her
eyes bore holes down the road as if she is clearing
a way ahead for us with her laser vision, and she
looks neither to left nor to right.

"What flowers? Never had much to do with
flowers. Dairy country in these parts. Good ice
cream."

I am surprised that someone so in tune with the
universe is not interested in its flowers but perhaps
she doesn't pay attention to such trivia because
she has big, important issues of good and bad energy to concentrate on. We stop at a small town to
buy cones and slurp them up as we drive along.

The ice cream is so full of fat it hardly drips. It's like eating a mound of flavored butter. What does melt slides down the cone in a creamy lather. This is like nothing I have eaten before and I begin to feel the stir of excitement in my rib cage of adventures to be had and I smile.

"Don't worry, child, we'll fix your bad energy," says Nellie, and that puts an end to my contentment.

We drive for a long time without a person to hand a Bible to. Then we come upon an old farmer walking down the road with his cows. I think the cows must have broken a fence somewhere and escaped and the farmer is taking them back. Either that or he takes them for walks the way some folks walk their dogs. It would be peaceful to walk some cows. They wouldn't bark alarmingly. They would moo in celestial harmony.

I am thinking this when Nellie stops the car suddenly, jolting me, and tries to hand the farmer a Bible out the window—we have a few on my lap at the ready. But the stopping of the car causes a ruckus with the cows, who begin to scatter in a frightened way that looks like the beginning of a stampede. The farmer waves us off with an irritated look. His peaceful cow walk has been disturbed. One of the cows brings its head too close to Nellie's window and she gets in a panic and puts the car in the wrong gear, which makes an awful, loud grinding sound, which further inflames the cows who begin to race around in six directions at once with the farmer shouting and flapping his arms and cursing us. Nellie finally gets the car out of there before we are run over by cows. The sound of the farmer's curses follows us down the road.

"He should have taken the Bible," Nellie says, panting. "Now, that's a man who could use a little positive energy." Sweat drips off her forehead. If I'd been killed by a cow it would have been hard to explain to my mother.

We drive on silently.

"I've never been in these parts," says Nellie after a while, breaking the comforting silence of the bubble that is our car moving through the stillness of the country afternoon.

We round a bend. I gasp. The field ahead of us looks like something out of a storybook. Giant balloons, all different, all in birthday-party colors. It is like being in someone's imagination.

"Can you see them too?" I ask, thinking maybe it is *my* imagination they are in. "Those things in the field?"

"Of course I can. They're right ding-dong there," says Nellie, who is beginning to look hot and cranky, pulling the car over to the side of the road with a thunk. "A bunch of hot-air balloons. You know what hot-air balloons are, don't you?"

"Hot-air balloons?" I say, breathing dizzily. Why has no one ever told me?

"Well, I expect you live in ignorance a fair amount of the time," says Nellie, sighing. "I always say to your mother that it's wrong cloistering you children like that down at the end of the beach where you're so sheltered from the world."

I think this is a strange way to look at it. As if, if we'd moved to town, the whole of mankind and its mysteries could *then* make its way to us and we'd know about everything that is. My best friend, Ginny, lives in our town's only new development. She has houses packed all around her and I know for sure she doesn't know everything there is. I envision the world coming to us, full of its hot-air balloons and countries and peoples and cities, all piling up in a giant mess at our doorstep. We'd never sort it out and all kinds of things would get broken and lost.

"See those baskets under the balloons? People *ride* in those," says Nellie.

"Do you think *we* could ride in one?" I ask Nellie. I pray right at that moment to get a chance. If I can, then I will let the universe off the hook for the other ninety-seven adventures it owes me.

"No time," says Nellie. "We've got important work ahead of us today."

She pauses a moment. "Those folks that are going up, though, they'll be covering a lot of territory, I'll be bound. Come on."

And then I see what she has in mind. She goes to the back of the station wagon and hauls out a box of Bibles, her knees nearly buckling under the weight. She bids me do the same and we trudge across the rutted field, getting bitten by bugs we are unable to swat.

"Now, what have we here?" asks one of the balloonists as we approach, but a kindly-looking lady says, "Shhh," and comes up to us. Nellie declares that she would like all the balloonists to take a few Bibles to distribute wherever their balloons take them, and that they can keep one for themselves to read on those long flights. One of the men starts laughing and the kindly woman puts her hand on his shoulder and tells him to go off and check some valves. Then she leads us over to a bright purple balloon, explaining that the balloons can't take a lot of extra weight.

"Maybe the two of you would like to get into the basket to see how it feels," she offers.

Nellie says she is too big and ungainly but that I'd probably like to. She frowns at me meaning-fully. I can't think why. She knows I'm dying to get into the basket.

The kindly lady explains the workings of the bal-loon to me and tells me to be careful of the burner, it is hot. She shows me how the port line is used to maneuver the balloon as it lands and how the blast valve gets the balloon up and how you make the balloon go down again. I keep hoping she will of-fer to take me for a ride but she doesn't. Never have I felt so much like a candle on a cake ready to be lit.

Instead, someone calls to her that they need help and she leaves us.

Nellie moves swiftly. She picks up a box of Bibles and goes around to the side of the balloon, which shields her from the others, and starts passing me Bibles. "Quick, quick, child, you just lay these in the bottom of that basket."

"Oh, Miss Phipps," I say. "It's no use. As soon as they get in, they'll just throw the Bibles out again. You may as well leave them lying in the field for all the good it will do."

"Hush, child, you do as I say," she hisses, busy passing them to me.

So I indulge her until nearly the whole bottom of the basket is full and then I say, "Besides, they told you it wasn't safe. The balloons can't take the extra weight. You don't want to endanger them."

"You don't weigh more than a feather, now do you?" asks Nellie. "We're just giving you a little necessary ballast. Now, you let those Bibles out over the houses as you go by."

"*ME?*" I squawk.

"Don't you get it? The universe has led us here," says Nellie.

I remember my prayer and how I wanted to

ride in a balloon. I should have asked for someone who knew what they were doing to be there
with me.

"Wait a second, Miss Phipps," I say. "I don't know
how to work this thing."

"You've got your valve and your port rope. You
heard the lady explain it. You'll do fine."

I want to say, Yeah, but what if I don't?, but it's
too late because Nellie has untied the last rope and
I am skyward bound.

Once I am aloft I am surprised how well I oper-
ate the balloon. I figure out the blast valve as I
move very slowly on currents of air. It is quiet and
peaceful and I wonder if I will be going to jail at
the end of this.

One of the first things I see from on high is Nellie running for all she is worth across the field with
a pack of angry balloonists after her, but they are
out of sight before I see the outcome. I am surprised by how fast Nellie can run.

I float above woods and fields serenely in the
quiet space between earth and sky, heaving Bibles
until I remember the backs of my family going
over that hill as though it were the last time I would

ever see them. Was that a premonition? I'm aw-fully high up.

This thought puts the brakes to the endeavor and I find a good field and maneuver the balloon down with a minimum of bumping and jerking. I am a natural balloonist but I doubt if anyone will be interested in this by the time they catch up with me. I am not surprised when I hear sirens and the sheriff appears.

But it is not me who goes to jail, it is Nellie. It turns out the sheriff had just dropped her off there when he got the call to pick me up. He tells me all about it as he drives me home. When he asked Nellie what in the world she was thinking, sending me up in a balloon, she insisted she was merely doing God's work, just like the saints. She told the sheriff he martyred her and asked if he planned to torture her too. He said he didn't own a rack but he could always bring her dinner from the Bluebird Café.

The sheriff gets a call from his office while we drive. They have already let Nellie out. The balloonists have decided not to press charges. The sheriff says he's glad and anyhow everyone knows church folks are simply crazy.

All my mother says when the sheriff drops me is "That Nellie Phipps." The sheriff tells my mother no one is blaming me. Nellie was the responsible adult. She was the brains of the outfit. Now that I am no longer eaten up by the desire to go for a balloon ride and can think straight, it occurs to me that I have kept all the balloonists from the day of ballooning they had planned. I ask the sheriff to please tell them how sorry I am.

Then the sheriff says he is glad no one is pressing charges because his wife is holding dinner for him.

Once he goes home I sit down and have clam chowder with my family. We are at the picnic table and the wind is blowing little salty blasts over our bowls. My mother says you don't need a saltshaker when you eat outdoors by the sea. Hershel says you don't need a sand shaker either, because sand has blown into his soup. My mother says she will get him a fresh bowl but he says don't bother, he likes the taste of sand.

"That's gross, Hershel," I say.

I tell them about the balloon ride. My mother says it's a miracle I wasn't hurt and I think she is right and then I remember gazing up at the balloon, a circle of purple light against the sky— the sign I had asked for. Goose bumps come up on my arms.

"What did you do in the balloon?" asks Maya.

"What was there to do but just ride?" I say. I don't mention dropping the Bibles.

The sea is turning bloodred in the sunset and I wonder what it means about the kind of week we have had. Even my mother says that it is a violent-looking sea. But all's well that ends well. Nellie Phipps got let out of jail so there's no reason to think this is a portent. It's just a sunset.

My mother passes me a bowl of strawberries.

"Enjoy them," she says. "They're the last of the season."

The Poetry Reading
My Fourth Adventure

The Raspberries Are Ripe

For five days nothing happens except summer. My adventures must be over because I have
gotten my balloon ride and that is the bargain I
have struck. But one morning a girl I don't know
comes over and I think hopefully that this may be
my next adventure beginning. She tells me she is a
page at the library. This throws me for a second. I
am thinking of all those book pages. Then I realize
that it is a job title. She has a note for my mother.
My mother has been out fishing from the pier on
the lake all morning because last night we had
chicken and rice for dinner without the chicken. I
take the note and sit on the porch waiting for her.
We have never gotten a hand-delivered note from

the library before and I want to know what it says
but it is sealed.

Finally my mother comes home with a small
bucket of perch and sits down next to me. "The
raspberries are ripe," she says. She holds out a small
cupful she has picked and we eat them together.
She smells earthy from digging worms and when
she opens her letter, she wipes a tendril of hair off
her forehead and out of her eyes in order to read,
leaving a dirty smudge.

"Well!" she says when she is done reading, and
folds the note up again. She stares into space for a
couple of minutes. Then she remembers I am there
and hands it to me.

It is from Mrs. Stewart, the librarian, saying they
are having a poetry reading at the library tonight
and three poets were to read but one has had to
cancel. The others are H. K. Thomson and Cassandra Lark. The library is offering my mother a
hundred dollars to come and read her poetry as
the replacement. I know she hates doing this. She
doesn't like being the center of attention. She says
it gives her the willies.

"Are you going to do it?" I ask.

"Yes," says my mother, sighing and getting up. "I'd better go prepare something. Could you take a note back to the library for me?"

She writes out an acceptance and as much as I know she doesn't want to do it I am glad because it has been five long days since the balloon ride and I am bored. I have reneged on my promise to God. I want my other ninety-seven adventures. I pray for them with renewed vigor.

I run across the sand barefoot and sit on a cement divider as I put on my sandals. People are piling out of cars to go down to the beach. I don't know any of them. A lot of them are probably tourists. They probably see our house and think how lucky we are.

I am walking past Dr. Callahan's office, which is next to the library, when I trip over one of the Gourd children. "Hey, watch it!" snaps Mrs. Gourd. She is coming down the doctor's steps with a baby carrier. There are little Gourds everywhere. The one I tripped over is crying so I put him back on his feet. Dr. Callahan waves at me from the top of the steps.

"Jane Fielding, look at you go!" he calls down.

"Tripping over children! Dropping Bibles out of balloons like missiles. When you kids in town start growing up and sowing your wild oats, why, you really sow them, now, don't you? You'd better be careful, Mrs. Gourd might sue next time!" He goes back inside.

Mrs. Gourd stands stock-still. She is thinking. Her eyes kind of roll when she does this. It is not the normal way a person thinks. It seems to require more mechanical effort. As if her eyes are needed to crank her brain into gear and keep it running. "You were dropping Bibles out of balloons like missiles? You're that hot-air-balloon girl."

"Why?" I ask. I really would like to forget the whole thing but she whips off the baby blanket that is covering the baby carrier and I gasp. There is a large purple lump on the top of the baby Gourd's head.

"That's why," she says grimly, and stares at me.

I just look at the bump dumbly for a minute while the little Gourd I tripped over wails.

"Well?" she demands finally.

"What do you mean?" I ask, but my mouth is dry even before my mind can form thoughts.

"I'll tell you what I mean, missy. I was walking with these children and one of them Bibles you was slinging out of that contraption hit my baby on the head and may have scarred him for life! That's what. He may never have no normal intelligence now."

"NO!" I say as the full implication of Dr. Callahan's words and what I have done comes over me. "NO!"

"Yes indeed. Now, just what're you planning on doing about that?"

One of the library clerks runs down the steps. "Hi, Jane, I hope your mom can read at the event tonight!" she calls to me as she dashes off. "I love her poetry!"

Mrs. Gourd's eyes go to the posters on the library door and windows about tonight's big poetry reading. "Which one is your mother?"

"My mother's Felicity Fielding but her name isn't on the poster because she is just substituting," I explain. Didn't I look *down* when I dropped the Bibles? Am I *crazy*? Didn't it occur to me I might *hit* someone?

"Well, well. I guess I better just show up at this

reading and see what she plans to do about her daughter maiming innocent babies. It's like the doctor said, I could sue, you know!"

I don't say anything and now she starts to smile and nod to herself in a satisfied manner. "Must be nice to be so rich that all you gotta do is write poetry all day. I gotta go make supper for Mr. Gourd right now but I'll be talking to your mama later and we'll just see about sharing some of that wealth."

Mr. Gourd is our school janitor and he scares me. He creeps around the hall with his mop and pail and a half-smoked cigarette always dangling from his lips. There are rumors that he has come to school drunk, that he has hit children, locked them in closets. I don't really believe these rumors but I don't want anything to do with him. Suppose my mother says no to Mrs. Gourd and Mr. Gourd comes to our house to try to talk to my mother. It will scare Max and Hershel and terrify Maya.

I think of last night and the bloodred sea. All has not ended well after all. I know what Nellie will say when she finds out. "I'm going straight to hell," I say, thinking aloud.

"You're going straight to jail first!" says Mrs.

Gourd indignantly as if I have tried to skip a step. She gathers up her children and leaves.

I look around. It has been as if everything, even time itself, had stopped during this debacle and now it has reset itself; people are once more walking by on their way to their various errands, their lives exactly where they left them when my life came to a crashing halt. For me things will never be the same. I have maybe injured a baby so seriously it will change his life and the life of his family forever. But overriding this is the terrible fear of my mother finding out, of her ruination on top of my own. I cannot let her find out about any of this.

Because I am thinking of my mother I make my way home, forgetting about the note, and when I get there, find it clutched in my hand, all sweaty and crumpled, and have to go back to the library, desperately aware of how little time I have left to come up with a plan.

Yesterday I was so full of hope. My life seemed blessed, full of adventures and answered prayers, and now something very, very bad has happened and it will never be the same again. And it all happened because I was greedy. Because I couldn't have an ordinary life. Because I was so taken with the wonders of the world that I could not be content with anything less than the constant awareness of its miracles. And you cannot have that in your basic nine-to-three schooltime routine, even with the best of teachers. Even with books to read. Even with the sound of the ocean every night. You need more.

"So," says Mrs. Stewart when I hand her my note. "She's saying yes for a change, is she?"

"Yes," I say breathlessly because my mind is racing ahead to my dim future. If we cannot pay what Mrs. Gourd wants, will I really be sent to jail? I see myself in a plain, round underground cement cell in which water drips on my head no matter where I stand and cockroaches are the size of birds and water bugs are the size of cats. But I have to eat them because they have forgotten my gruel tray again. And then for a change of pace I go to hell.

Mrs. Stewart makes a face that is kind of a sneer and kind of triumphant. "Well, I guess she sees she has to do this sort of thing now and then," she says, making another mean face. I don't know why she is so mad at my mother. "I'll put her on in the middle between Cassandra and H.K. They're both experienced at this sort of thing. Tell your mother we'll need about twenty minutes is all. If she's got it. I'll give H.K. and Cassandra the bulk of the evening as that's who people are coming to see."

I nod and head home. For a moment I formulate a plan to tell my mother that the library has changed its mind and she needn't do the reading. But she will just find out I lied and Mrs. Gourd will track us down at home. Besides, now we need every penny to pay her off.

When I get in I tell my mother that Mrs. Stewart said she needs twenty minutes.

"Goodness, is that all? Thank heavens," my mother says. "Can you watch Maya and Max and Hershel for me if I bring them along?"

I nod.

"Are you feeling well, Jane?"

I nod again. She looks at me searchingly as if to discover what has besieged me and fix it but all she can think to say is "Maybe Ginny would like to come with us?"

For the first time since I talked to Mrs. Gourd I

feel a stab of relief. Ginny is smart and clearheaded and practical. But even more important, she is always on my side. She already knows what she wants to do with her life. She is going to be a dress designer in New York City. She has it all thought out. If anyone can help me come up with a plan to circumvent Mrs. Gourd, it is Ginny.

My mother sees how happy this thought has made me and she says, "Well, for heaven's sakes. Run and get her now. She can have dinner with us."

I run across the sand to the development where Ginny lives. I weave my way through the new roads with their black asphalt and crisp sidewalks edged by fresh-cut grass. Ginny's house is neat. The garage is large and in front of the house and gapes at you. Our house stands guard over us but Ginny's feels like a soft plush monster that swallows you into the comfort of its great carpeted maw. Everything is so soft you do not even know you have been divided from all that is alive. You cannot feel the wind or cold or damp. There are no hard surfaces or sharp sounds. There is no danger here. Streetlights outside her window keep light always around, inside and out. This artificial light pretends that here there is only safety and life, but this light itself is a kind of death. It is death to the deep night.

Ginny answers the door. Her mother and father are at work. She takes me up to her room. The walls are slick with shiny wallpaper. She has bunk beds. I always thought I would sleep in one if I slept over but I have never been invited. Ginny has never said so but I think her mother is somehow suspicious of my family and the way we live on the beach.

I begin to feel that I cannot breathe. I feel caged. The soft, quieting carpeting makes me crazy for the sound of the sea.

"Can you come to my house for supper? Can you leave your mother a note?"

"What's the matter with you?" Ginny asks, but I cannot talk in this smothering place.

She writes a note to her mother and we run until we are someplace where I can see the wind moving the trees. Where I feel the universe at work again. Then I sit and tell Ginny everything that has happened.

"Oh no," she says, putting her hand to her mouth

in horror. This is why I like Ginny. She does not try to talk you out of the gravity of the situation.

She does not remove her hand from her mouth but says through it, "You've been busy since I last talked to you." It is inestimably comforting to have a friend, someone who is not horrified at you but with you.

"It's all so terrible and it all started because Mrs. Parks had a thrombosis and it wasn't interesting like Mrs. Nasters's cancer."

"Mrs. Nasters has cancer?" asks Ginny. In the midst of so much horror, it is good to catch up. I have been in such crazy places alone in my head the last few days and our ordinary, familiar talk helps to steady me. Mrs. Nasters lives next door to Ginny but no one has told Ginny about the cancer. Ginny's parents never tell her anything they think might be upsetting for children. I explain how taking Mrs. Parks's side prayerwise led to a series of events that begat my downfall.

"Everyone is always telling us to make good choices," says Ginny. "But how can you know what a good choice is until you see the results and when so much can go wrong from just one unthinking thing?"

I start to say something but am interrupted.

"She could take your house!" says Ginny. She knows how important our house is.

This has not occurred to me and now I begin to shake.

"All right, all right, calm down. She wants your mother to make an offer but we can't let your mother know anything, I agree." She puts a steadying hand on my forearm. "We have to make an offer first and we have to make it before Mrs. Gourd gets to your mother tonight."

My mother seems outwardly calm at dinner. She does everything the same, puts dishes on the table and talks to us as normal and looks out in her usual stillness at the waves. When Horace comes barking over and races around under the picnic table begging food, she just picks him up and holds him on her lap, stroking him gently and suggesting that he won't much like what we're eating, otherwise we'd share, until Mrs. Spinnaker comes and roughly grabs him out of her hands. Then instead of striding purposefully off as usual, Mrs. Spinnaker turns and eyes my mother speculatively and says, "I hear you're going to do a reading at the library tonight. That's you, isn't it, Felicia Fielding? I saw your name inked over someone else's on the library poster." It always seems strange to hear my mother's whole name. The name on her books.

"Yes," says my mother.

"Humph," says Mrs. Spinnaker. "Taken up a little writing, have you? Well, we all have our hobbies. I do crosswords."

It's hard to know how to respond to this. She's got that poor dog like a football under her arm and it looks to me as if she's crushing him but he has a resigned expression on his face as if he's used to it and knows if he keeps quiet he will eventually be set down.

"Here, let me get you one of my books," says my mother, slipping out from the picnic table and going into the house, but Mrs. Spinnaker ambles back to her cottage, talking to Horace all the way.

My mother doesn't come back out with the poetry book and when Ginny and I go inside is washing the dishes. "I saw her leaving from the kitchen window," she says in explanation, shaking her head and smiling. "I wonder if she is coming to the reading."

"Do you want her to?" I ask.

"I don't like anyone I know to be there," says my mother.

"Except us children, right?" I say.

"Especially not anyone who knows me well. But, of course, H.K. will already be there so you children may as well be too."

I wait for her to explain what she means but she doesn't, she just goes on dreamily washing pans and gazing out at the wish-wash swish-swash of the waves. I wonder if she has lost track of her hands in the dishwater and thinks they are swimming in their own frothy sea but Ginny has another idea. She pulls me into my bedroom and whispers, "What does she mean H.K. knew her *well*? What does a woman mean when she says a man knew her *well*? It means he was her boyfriend, right?"

"Oh!" I say, and suddenly remember to tell her about the clothes hanger man.

"Are you sure she used the words 'your father'?" Ginny asks when I'm done.

"How could I have misunderstood? I was standing right next to her."

"She didn't say Oh, what a bother? Or Well, yes,
but I'd rather? Or Yes, so I gather?"

I scan back but I cannot think. Too much has
happened since then.

"And how could H.K. have been a boyfriend
without you seeing him around? Did you ever see
any men around?"

"No," I say.

"And yet there must have been."

"Stop it!" I say, and am surprised by the vehe-
mence in my voice.

So is Ginny. "Well, anyhow, I think you heard
wrong about this clothes hanger man. If your mother
were to tell you, she would never say it so casually."

But it is exactly the type of thing my mother
would do. I know Ginny doesn't understand. No
one really understands a family but the people in it
and even they each understand it differently.

My mother calls that it is time to leave. Only
when we arrive at the library does she begin to
look nervous. One hand shakes slightly as she
picks up a flyer about the reading. It talks mainly
about H.K. and his workshops at colleges and his

grants and awards. My mother has won a Pulitzer but it doesn't mention this. Only that she is replacing the third poet, who couldn't come.

"Why don't they mention your Pulitzer?" I ask.

"Maybe because it was so long ago," says my mother. "Maybe because it makes them angry that I usually say no to readings. They think I'm snotty, maybe. It doesn't matter, Jane." She leaves us to sit at the front.

Ginny and I have Maya and Hershel and Max in the back and things are about to start. My mother has put a stack of picture books by them and seated us where they can play on the floor with the tiny toy trucks she brought for Hershel and Max. Maya has her paper dolls. I think the trucks are a mistake. Max and Hershel like to make vroom vroom sounds when the trucks go. I tell them they will have to stop that when the readings begin but I know they will forget. I keep looking for Mrs. Gourd but she isn't there.

I am beginning to think it will all be okay after all, when Ginny leaps up. She points out the big picture windows that form one wall of the library. "There she is!" she croaks hoarsely in my ear, and goes racing outside, where Mrs. Gourd, surrounded by little Gourds and holding the baby carrier, is talking to an assistant librarian on the front steps. Through the window I see Ginny pretending to kneel and tie her shoe. Then the assistant librarian goes inside and Ginny grabs Mrs. Gourd and begins talking to her. I am amazed at how bold Ginny can be with grown-ups. I am relieved that she might talk Mrs. Gourd out of suing.

I keep staring at them out the window although Mrs. Stewart has gone to the front of the room.

"Welcome to a very special evening at the library," she begins.

"Vroom vroom," goes Max.

Mrs. Stewart looks around, trying to figure out where that sound is coming from.

"I'd like to welcome all of you and especially our honored poets, who—"

"Vroom," goes Hershel.

"Shhh," I say.

Mrs. Stewart looks at me and frowns. I look at Max and frown. Max starts to crawl toward the window. I get down and crawl after him, trying to hide behind chairs so Mrs. Gourd, if she glances inside, won't see me.

Mrs. Gourd has her hands on her hips and looks

angry but I think she may be one of those people who always looks angry. Ginny is gesticulating and the Gourd children are racing wildly over the steps and we can hear them and the baby crying.

"Marian, can you please go outside and see what is going on," says Mrs. Stewart, sending the assistant librarian into the fray. "As I was saying, it's a great pleasure to have a poet like H. K. Thomson here with us tonight." But many heads are still turned toward the steps, where the assistant librarian is talking to Mrs. Gourd.

Ginny races back in and plops herself next to me. I don't dare say anything. Mrs. Stewart is staring at the two of us as if we will be ejected any minute. But, then, oh thank heavens, Mrs. Gourd leaves. I see her snap something at the Gourd children, who immediately stop running around and follow her down the steps.

"Well, let us delay no longer. I'm so pleased to introduce tonight a poet all of you know. She graces many of our town's events and gives generously of her time—please welcome Cassandra Lark."

There is some mild applause. Max and Hershel are still whispering "Vroom" but fortunately Cassandra Lark takes the podium with such drama, so many swishy black layers and beads, and she shouts her poetry so loudly that it commands our attention again.

When she is finished and while everyone is applauding, Ginny tells me what has happened. She has told Mrs. Gourd that we will meet her in the parking lot by the beach tomorrow morning to make an offer. Ginny doesn't let Mrs. Gourd know that my mother won't be there. Also, the assistant librarian has told Mrs. Gourd that it might not be a good idea to bring a crying baby and all the little Gourds to a poetry reading.

"This is fortunate because she seemed pretty determined to talk to your mother," says Ginny. "But by tomorrow, we will have a plan."

Then Mrs. Stewart introduces my mother. My mother's voice is calm and quiet and when she starts reading, her nervous face gives way to one that is full of wonder for the things she has written about. She does not punch her words like Cassandra Lark or look as if she is listening to her voice more than reading to us. The words roll. She looks plain in a way that is beautiful. The way Shaker furniture is beautiful.

I do not listen to any poetry. I keep going through the events of the day over and over. I just want to go home and go to bed now that the adrenaline has stopped coursing through me, but H. K. Thomson takes an entire hour. Finally it is over and the librarian thanks the poets but she is looking only at H. K. Thomson and then she talks about upcoming library business and everyone convenes for cake and coffee.

Ginny doesn't want any cake. She says she will go home and try to figure out what to say to Mrs. Gourd in the morning and I walk her down the library steps, making plans for her to knock on my window at dawn.

I go back inside to find my mother. I realize I have left Maya and Hershel and Max and I was supposed to be watching them. I look worriedly for them now but they are fine. They are gathered around the refreshment table, where they are messily eating cake. As long as there is cake on the table they will be happily occupied. Chocolate frosting is smeared all over Hershel's face. I bend over to pick up their toys and put them back in the plastic bag. At that moment I spy my mother, who is talking to H. K. Thomson. He is listening to her but looking at Max and Hershel and Maya with horror. I know they are messy but horror seems like an extreme reaction.

H.K.'s sister, Caroline, is sitting alone in a folding chair among a sea of empty chairs, glaring at my mother. Maybe she wants to get home and thinks my mother is delaying H.K. My mother keeps talking and H.K. is looking ill. Maybe he has eaten too much cake.

I go over to get my mother. I am exhausted by everything and full of dread. I stand by her and grab her sweater and she reaches down and takes my hand without looking at me.

"Anyhow, I thought perhaps you should know. I wouldn't have said anything if you hadn't made that remark about how adorable the children were."

"This is quite a shock, Felicity. But don't worry, I will do the right thing."

"Don't be silly, Henry. There's no need to do anything at all."

"We must talk about this some more. Let's do lunch."

My mother laughs and then looks at his face and sees he is serious. "Well, of course, if that's what you'd like. Certainly. I'd be happy to have lunch sometime. Now I really must get home. Hershel is going to get chocolate on everything before long and Delores has had quite enough of us, I can see."

She means Mrs. Stewart, who is shooing Max and Maya and Hershel in the direction of the door while trying to keep their sticky fingers off her.

My mother and I hurry Hershel and Maya and Max the rest of the way out of the building. My mother thanks the librarian, who just nods curtly and runs off toward H.K.

We reach the beach. The wind picks up and I take off my shoes. The sand is comfortingly cool on my hot feet. I run down the beach for the wind in my face and my hair. I feel the way the birds must when they are blown about on its currents. When I run back to my mother I am better even though I know it is only temporary.

My mother laughs at me but doesn't say much. She laughs easily and at nothing now that the reading is over. We all walk looking out to sea. It is crashing in the evening light, great splashing white horses running over the sand.

"What were you and H. K. Thomson talking about?" I ask.

"He told me he hadn't read any of my books. He said he's sorry but he will try to get around to it sometime," says my mother, and then erupts in peals of laughter. It falls across the summer twilight like bells.

And suddenly I think of the Christmas Eve when my mother and I were to help Nellie Phipps ring our church's bells at exactly midnight. Nellie watched the time but suddenly the bells of the other church in town, St. Matthew's, started pealing and she grabbed the ropes frantically. She mustn't be late, she said, charged with this sacred duty. She rang so hard and so fast to catch up that her efforts didn't seem humanly possible and my mother and I watched her in awe, not even touching the ropes. "God help me. God help me," Nellie said, and it looked as if her prayers were answered because she no longer needed us. When we had practiced earlier in the day it had taken three of us on a rope. Now she was pulling both ropes herself. My mother put a hand on my shoulder as if protecting me from something that could not be explained.

I remind my mother of this. How maybe it was an indication of Nellie's mysticism.

"What I always wondered was why it never occurred to her that St. Matthew's was simply ring-
ing their bells too early," says my mother.

Now within the roar of the surf and the roar of
the wind we are surrounded by something so sonorous it presses out all thought. Even this new
idea about Nellie. It is like being within the sound
of the bells again. How do people live who do not
live by the sea? How do people live without this
sonorous presence? Then we are at the house and
my feet feel the welcoming painted wood floors of
the porch and I know the sonorous thing is in our
porch floors too. My feet reach for it.

"It's always good to come home," says my mother,
sighing, and she picks up Hershel and carries him
into the house, his chocolate mouth resting against
her clean white blouse.

The Rescue

My Fifth Adventure

I am awoken by Ginny tapping on the window. I get up and raise the window sash and she climbs in.

"I have an idea," she says.

We go down the hall to the kitchen. My mother has been up picking raspberries and the kitchen smells like raspberry muffins. There is a basket of them on the kitchen table. There are a jam jar of roses and a pitcher of milk next to the muffins. My mother has a pot of raspberry jam started on the stove. She has been busy already by daybreak.

I suddenly wonder where the roses came from. We have none growing around our house and that is when I see my mother and H. K. Thomson sitting on the beach, talking.

"What's he doing here?" Ginny asks.

"I think he's taking my mother to lunch," I say.

"But it's breakfast time," says Ginny.

We sit down and eat muffins with an open jar of my mother's strawberry jam. There is a whole row of them in the pantry. Then Maya comes in looking all sleepy and we pour her a glass of milk and put a muffin on a plate for her.

"What's your idea?" I ask Ginny.

She empties her pockets onto the kitchen table. "My quarters from my New York jar," she says. Because Ginny wants to be a dress designer when she grows up, she is saving up her spare quarters to go to New York and scope things out. She says she may go to dress designer college or she may just muscle her way into the business. She is thinking about it still, and planning.

"That's your New York money," I say, and put another muffin on each of our plates.

"Not anymore," says Ginny.

Maya brings Ginny pen and paper and while Ginny talks she draws beautiful, fantastic outfits for Maya's paper dolls.

"Now, listen," Ginny goes on. She leans on the table with one forearm and puts her face close to mine, staring me hard in the eye. "Here is how we stave off Mrs. Gourd. When we meet her in the parking lot, we give her all my New York money as a down payment and we tell her we will keep paying her off so long as she tells absolutely no one about the dropped Bible. Then we just find jobs, is all."

I am touched by Ginny's giving up her quarters for me as much as I am aware that this is just one more person whose life I have potentially derailed.

I get changed quickly with Maya clinging to Ginny and begging her not to leave. Maya stands pathetically with her face pressed against the screen door but we turn our backs and run across the sand.

The air smells this morning like it has just come out of the wash. The sun is still low, casting white, opaque light. The ocean is quiet but beginning to whoosh as if it is getting in gear for the things it has planned for our day. As if it is time's great internal-combustion engine. The mist patches run across the wet sand, late to work. It is commuting mist.

We sit on the cement dividers all morning and

Mrs. Gourd still does not come. We have not taken sunscreen because somehow I thought Mrs. Gourd was coming at daybreak. Like the gunfight at the O.K. Corral. It is past noon when we see her old green station wagon pull up. All the little Gourds are in tow, armed with sand toys. They are already slapping each other with their shovels. The baby makes not a peep. It has a blanket over its carrier again. I wonder if this is like riding in a litter.

Mrs. Gourd looks like she is going right past us and down to the beach but Ginny stops her with a raised hand.

"Mrs. Gourd!" she calls. "I have a proposition."

There is a man sitting on a cement divider in another part of the parking lot and he looks up with curiosity. He has been sitting there for the last ten minutes smoking cigarettes as if he, like us, is waiting for someone. But now when he looks at us it is as if he is satisfied; he was just waiting for *something* and all of us are as good as anything.

Mrs. Gourd stops and looks at Ginny. "A what?" she asks.

Ginny gets out her two handfuls of quarters. "These are for you," she says.

"What for?" asks Mrs. Gourd but before she gets the answer, takes and pockets them.

"For your baby," Ginny says. "Instead of going to see Mrs. Fielding, why don't you deal directly with us? Mrs. Fielding has no money anyway."

"You again!" Mrs. Gourd says to Ginny. "You in that contraption dropping Bibles with this one?" She points at me.

"I am Jane's friend," says Ginny. Everything is in this statement. "We will make payments until we pay off whatever you and Jane decide is fair. The only thing is, you can't tell Mrs. Fielding or *anyone* anything about the baby. If you do, we get all our money back."

"Where you going to get the money?" asks Mrs. Gourd. She puts the baby carrier down and stares challengingly at us.

"We'll get jobs," says Ginny.

"Pfff," says Mrs. Gourd, picking up the baby carrier again and letting her eyes drop to me. They are like knives. "You can't get no jobs."

"We'll get babysitting jobs," says Ginny. "I've had the Red Cross babysitting course. You can make a lot of money babysitting."

Mrs. Gourd looks out over the sand. Her eyes start doing that thing again, moving back and forth, cranking her brain into gear.

"Babysitting?" she says.

"Uh-huh," says Ginny.

Mrs. Gourd's eyes dart, dart. "You babysit for me," she says.

"WHAT?" cries Ginny. She eyes those smelly, runny Gourd children.

"That's what I said. You babysit for me. I want that job coming open at the Bluebird Café. That waitress job. You babysit for me and I'll think about letting you pay off the debt this way. For now."

"I don't know," says Ginny. "How many hours a day is that? We've got school in the fall, you know."

"Well, we worry about that in the fall," says Mrs. Gourd. Her mouth is closing in kind of a happy smile like she has opened chocolates and found one she likes. That is when I notice that among her other difficulties she has one long, yellow snaggle-tooth that sticks out from under her upper lip and sort of hangs there, threatening to pierce her lower lip. I can see her using it to poke holes in chocolates to suck out the filling and see if she likes it. She barks at me, "YOU'D BETTER," as if I were thinking of saying no, and I can't tell her I was just staring at the snaggle-tooth.

"Oh, I *will*," I say. I will promise anything if she just doesn't talk to my mother. If she just doesn't sue us.

I can't figure out whether the man with the cigarettes is close enough to hear us. I realize suddenly the importance of keeping this whole thing contained. So far only Dr. Callahan, Ginny, Mrs. Gourd and I know what I have done, although it feels as if everyone in town knows. As if it is written all over me. It was an accident. It was really Nellie's fault. I explain this mentally to people over and over.

I search for signs that the cigarette man has overheard us but he isn't looking our way while he smokes, although his ears are perked like a dog's. He gets into his car and drives away. Who comes to the beach just to sit in the parking lot and smoke?

Mrs. Gourd grabs me by the chin and swings my face back around toward her. "You start now. I won't tell no one about what you done or what's it done to Willie Mae and you don't tell no one about our deal either. You tell someone and it's off and I will go get my fancy lawyer to talk to your mother and then it's all up with you, ain't it?"

She puts the baby carrier in my hand and gives Ginny the diaper bag and then she starts to stump back toward her car.

Ginny and I run after her. We don't even know the children's names, we say. The Gourd children go wild and start running all over the beach. Mrs. Gourd points out Darsie, Dee Dee, Darvon and Dean. I wonder if she ran out of D names when she got to Willie Mae or just got tired of them.

"Wait a second," yells Ginny. "When are you getting back? What do we feed them?"

"You take them on back to the trailer and give them peanut butter and jelly when they get hungry but don't take none for yourself. I ain't a restaurant. Baby's bottle is in the diaper bag and there's an extra in the fridge," says Mrs. Gourd, and then gets in her car, and the tires squeal as she pulls away.

I am so relieved it has been this easy that I

almost faint. At the same time I worry that we are just delaying the inevitable. That eventually we will be caught.

"I'm sorry about your quarters," I say to Ginny. "I'm sorry about everything."

"There's something not right here," says Ginny. "She leapt on that deal too fast."

But we have no time to think about it because the Gourd children have seen that their mother has left and are going crazy on the beach, running into the water and in all different directions, and we have a terrible time roping them in. Then Ginny teaches me how to change a diaper and what to do if a child is choking and other things she has learned in her course. It helps to pass the time, which moves more slowly than you would think possible. As if it is being weighted by all those Gourd children.

"Do we have to do this for the rest of our lives, do you think? Does she plan to have us always babysit?" I ask as I get Darvon in one hand and Darsie in the other.

"Well," says Ginny, panting and grabbing Dean by the shirt, "eventually they have to grow up."

It is a long, exhausting afternoon but by four o'clock we have a rule that works. When we say drop everything, the Gourd children have to freeze, and they aren't allowed to move until we touch them. We make a game of this. I cannot help feeling this is going to work only until they get tired of the game but it is enough for now. They are hungry and Dee Dee hits Darvon.

"All of you follow me. We are taking you home and feeding you peanut butter," says Ginny. She doesn't talk to them in the sweet voice she uses for Max and Hershel and Maya. They trail her in a bedraggled line, too tired to be wild anymore.

The trailer door is standing wide open. The children run joyfully in and I am appalled at their audacity before I realize that it is their home and of course they don't need to knock. They are so filthy and matted that I can't imagine them having a home that they love the way we do ours. And maybe they don't love home. Maybe they just love peanut butter.

They are all over the trailer and Ginny makes them sandwiches while I pour Kool-Aid. There is peanut butter smeared and dried on a lot of the furniture and my guess is they eat a lot of it. We cannot find the jelly but they don't seem to notice. I hear a sound and it makes me jump and I realize that Mr. Gourd is sleeping in the next room. He is snoring loudly and thrashing around. Why couldn't he watch them if he is here all day?

Just then Mrs. Gourd comes in. She looks at their sandwiches. "I thought I told you to make them peanut butter and *jelly,*" she says to Ginny, who is putting the bread away.

"I couldn't find any," says Ginny calmly, but there is an edge to her voice. I imagine her duking it out mano a mano with Mrs. Gourd. Ginny is young and muscular but Mrs. Gourd is mean. It would be an interesting match.

"Well, that's just fine. I suppose you mean for them children to develop vitamin deficiencies. That there jelly is their *fruit,*" Mrs. Gourd says, pointing to the recommended fruit and vegetable portion of the government food pyramid stuck to the fridge.

"Jelly is not a fruit," says Ginny. I'd better get her home. She has clearly had it.

Mrs. Gourd reaches up on the top shelf of one of the grimy cupboards and pulls down a sticky old jar. She shoves it right in Ginny's face, pointing to the word APPLE. "You look right here, APPLES. Are you telling me that apples aren't fruit?"

"Oh, for Pete's sake," says Ginny, starting for the door. I follow her.

"I expect to see you girls bright and early tomorrow morning. Yep. Bright and early, because I got the job and I'll be working nine till three," says Mrs. Gourd. She smirks but she looks proud.

As we leave we hear Mr. Gourd's voice. He has woken up. He yells at Mrs. Gourd. The children start wailing.

"Well, there's no question who fathered *those* children," says Ginny as Mr. Gourd and his children harmonize their loud noises. I pretend not to know what she means and then we see a peanut butter jar come flying out the window and we spontaneously break into a run and keep running until we get close to town.

"That was awful," says Ginny, panting, as we slow down on the corner where she'll split off for her street. "That sound he made. I've never heard anyone yell at someone like that."

"Ginny . . . ," I say.

"This is a horrible predicament," she says grimly, "but it's not your fault," and turns toward her street without a backward glance.

When I get to the parking lot there is the man with the cigarettes, sitting on a cement divider, smoking and staring down the beach. He pretends not to look at me but I can see he is sneaking glances in my direction. In fact, I can feel his eyes bore their way into the back of my neck as I walk across the parking lot. I pass his car. It has an Ontario license plate. I look at him again. I have never seen a Canadian, at least as far as I know. What is he doing here? Maybe his life is so empty all he has to do is slowly migrate south, smoke and study people. He has seen me three times now so I guess he thinks of me as a regular. He has a nice face, in sort of a distracted way, and I begin to study it but just then I see H.K. heading toward me. Don't tell me he has been at our house the whole day! What could he and my mother possibly have to say to each other for so long? H.K's face is in contemplation too but it is not nice, it is closed up tight and he is somewhere so deep inside you will never be invited in.

At home, my mother is humming and setting the table. She has summer tomatoes on the stove cooking down for spaghetti sauce, which she says she is putting on rice because we are out of spaghetti. We have a huge fifty-pound bag of rice that she bought ages ago. It is only half empty so we will have many more rice dinners, I suppose.

"I saw Mr. Thomson," I say. "Was he here all day?"

"Yes. Troubled man. He is trying to work something out where there is nothing to be worked out," she says. "Can you set the table, Jane?"

I take down the mismatched plates and start to put them on the picnic table, but a terrible sound comes from down the beach and we all race there to find Mrs. Spinnaker standing, staring at the horizon and screaming. Horace has been swept out to sea by a wave too big for him. Mrs. Spinnaker, who doesn't swim, is hopping up and down on the beach yelling, "Save him! Oh, save him!" There is no one else here and she does not see us approaching. She is calling to the universe.

My mother calmly takes off her long skirt and runs into the surf in her underpants and T-shirt and starts to swim. The tide is going out and there must be a current; it keeps pulling my mother sideways. Horace is bobbing. Sometimes we don't see him as he disappears, and then Mrs. Spinnaker screams. My mother is not swimming hard and then I see why not. She is trying to let the current take her toward Horace and I know she is saving her strength for the swim back. They are a long way out. Finally we see her grab him but now I am worried about her. She is going to have to swim against the current to get back to shore and she is just a dot.

"Whales!" says Max, who has come out of the house with Hershel and Maya.

"That is Mama," I say, and then we are all quiet. Everyone is clasping their hands and no one is saying a word.

It takes my mother a very long time to make it back against the current and the tide and when at long last she comes upright, she is unsmiling. Horace is shaking and miserable-looking but alive. She hands him to Mrs. Spinnaker, who has a towel ready and wraps Horace quickly in it and runs back to her cottage with him. My mother sits down right there in the sand, with her wet hair plastered to her face.

I remember the spaghetti sauce and run back inside. The bottom of it is burnt. I turn the burner off and put some rice on to cook. I have never made rice before but I have seen my mother do it a million times.

My mother comes in finally and takes a shower to clean off the salt and sand and warm herself up and by the time she is done I have dinner on the table. She looks at me and touches my shoulder as she takes her place. "I am so lucky," she says.

The Seer

My Sixth Adventure

It is Sunday again. Just as we have finished cleaning up and getting the boys into their better shirts, there is a knock on the door. It is H. K. Thomson and my mother does not seem surprised to see him. He is wearing a bow tie and has a carnation in the buttonhole of his seersucker jacket. My mother greets him calmly and continues gathering the boys' shoes and then we are out the door. He is going to church with us. I have seen him at church often with his sister, Caroline, but she is not with him now.

It is a morning of sea breezes and mists on the beach and we run down it, leaving my mother to walk with H. K. Thomson. It is good to run in my dress. I like the feel of my bare legs moving freely in a way they can't in pants. I think it is sad that men never get to feel this. Except Scottish men with their kilts. The boys don't seem to care about being so imprisoned, perhaps because they have never known the freedom of legs in a skirt. Their cuffs are full of sand when they get to the parking lot and we have to dump them as well as their shoes. H.K. doesn't take his shoes off to dump the sand and looks vaguely irritated at the delay while we all desand ourselves meticulously.

Once we are free of sand we run down Main Street to our little white-steepled church. It is packed. A lot has happened this week and everyone wants to get a load of Nellie Phipps, preacher and jailbird. But she acts as if nothing unusual has happened until she gets to her sermon and then she makes references to jail and being threatened with dinner from the Bluebird Café and Jesus and his crown of thorns, none of which makes sense thrown together like that unless you happen to know about the incident with the balloons. She mixes the two up so that it sounds as if Jesus had supper at the Bluebird Café. I imagine him signing

a picture for their wall like the other local celebri-
ties. H. K. Thomson's picture hangs in there. My
mother's picture does not.

People are beginning to purse their lips and look
uncomfortable. You can tell that the ones who
don't know about Nellie's brief jail time think she
is rambling in a disturbing way. There is a sense of
relief when it is time to pray for the sick.

We pray for Mrs. Nasters and Mrs. Parks again.
Mrs. Nasters is getting worse but Mrs. Parks is getting better. I have the terrible thought that maybe
my prayer tipped the balance, the extra prayer for
Mrs. Parks, that is, the omission of the prayer for
Mrs. Nasters. My mind wanders along worrying
about this. And I realize that we have been so busy
that none of us has checked up again on Mrs. Parks
since our adventure with her. This seems a little
mean. You don't want to be the type of person who
only shows up during a crisis. As if you are just
hunting for excitement. I decide I will go visit her
today. And also Mrs. Nasters because I owe her
that much. Even though she may think it peculiar
since I don't know her very well.

I am passing behind H. K. Thomson and my
mother as we exit the church, hoping to slide out

under cover of their bulk, but Nellie Phipps grabs my hand purportedly to shake it and draws me near and whispers in my ear. "Not so fast. We got Bibles to give away, don't forget."

"Oh, Nellie, not after last week," I say. She doesn't know what terrible thing has happened and I cannot tell her in front of all these people.

"Child, especially after last week. I've got your spiritual health to tend to. Now, don't fret about sending me to jail. That was just a blip. Go tell your mother you'll be gone all day. I got a route all picked out."

I do not know what to do. I can't say no to a grown-up, especially a preacher. I am counting on my mother to save me. I snag her as she is inviting Caroline to Sunday dinner. I can't tell if Caroline has understood my mother. Her hair is all wild and her eyes are looking crazy and angry. My mother appears distracted as I tell her that I am going to deliver Bibles while my eyes plead with her to say that I can't. But before she can say anything, H. K. Thomson says, "Come along, Felicity. It looks as if Jane is going to be busy and Caroline has other plans for supper," and shepherds her away.

I stand openmouthed with Nellie's hand still

gripping mine. She holds it with her right, which forces her to shake hands with her left. It puts her so out of balance she cannot kiss any babies. I think the mothers look glad.

Caroline is the last person to depart. She has been sitting in the corner of a pew staring at nothing. Nellie putters around the church putting things away but she is keeping a sharp eye on me at all times as if I am an untethered horse. Finally, she signals that she is ready to go and we march to the parking lot. The Bibles are already in the back of the station wagon. I am hungry for lunch and wonder if we will stop for ice cream again and if we will be back in time for me to visit Mrs. Parks and Mrs. Nasters, because I can't see them during the week. I will be babysitting.

"Stealing a balloon to deliver Bibles is not the same as regular stealing," says Nellie as we drive down the road.

I don't say anything. I don't want to talk any more about positive and negative energies and how I am making mistakes.

Then Nellie's face clears as if she has thought of something new. "Your mother had better watch her step. Yep. I'd say your mother'd better watch her step, all right."

"What do you mean?"

"Well, you don't mean to tell me you've never heard that Caroline took an axe to H.K.'s last girlfriend."

"She hit her with an AXE?"

"Well, of course, to hear Caroline tell it, that leg was ready to come off by itself."

"What happened?"

"Sixteen stitches and Caroline went back into the loony bin, where everyone thinks she always belonged anyway. That rich old family and all they produce are a poet and a loony toon woman who can get a PhD but not a job and so H.K. has to take care of her. I'd say Caroline's energies are definitely blocked."

"I thought she was keeping house for H.K.," I say.

"That's what they'd have you believe," says Nellie. "But anyway, he's not what I'd consider an eligible bachelor. Not unless you're *very* swift-moving."

I don't say anything.

"Anyhow, I hope you don't think I'm criticizing your mother. There aren't a lot of men her age available, I would guess."

"My mother is not H.K.'s girlfriend. She's just helping him through some troubles," I say.

"If that's what she told you, then I'm sure it's true," says Nellie.

"She told me she's just helping him during a hard time."

Nellie doesn't say anything or move her eyes from the road but her lips start working in a worried, irritated way as if this is something she hadn't counted on and now she is going to have to rethink things and she doesn't like not knowing everything but she can't disagree with me without contradicting my mother. So to change the subject I tell her about the Gourd baby even though I had planned to tell no one but Ginny. I don't even like thinking about it and when I say that I may have maimed him for life I begin shaking slightly.

Nellie stops the car right there and turns and looks at me. A long look as if she has to size me up all over again. Then she says, "We must not judge." She drives on and then she says, "Of course, you're

in the soup energy-wise. But there are no acci-
dents. Maybe that baby was meant to be maimed
or maybe you were meant to have this horrific occurrence that changes your future."

We drive quietly for a long time and then a ways
out of town we skid suddenly to a gravelly stop.
There is a garish trailer parked by the side of the
road and a sign on it saying MADAME CRENSHAW.
YOUR FUTURE'S IN YOUR HANDS.

"This must be it. We're making a little stop here,"
Nellie says briefly. She doesn't get a Bible out of
the back.

"Why?" I ask as we walk to the door of the
trailer.

"I heard some things about this woman. From
Mabel next door. She had her fortune told. She
says this fortune-teller is gifted. She has the sight.
We'll check it out and see if it's true. I want to ask
her about what you need for absolution."

"I'm already babysitting," I say.

"Well, maybe she can see down the years. How
it all pans out. If that baby recovers."

I am game to do this even though I don't want to
start relying on fortune-tellers in garish trailers.

But I want to keep an open mind after seeing Nellie with Mrs. McCarthy. The universe is full of wonders and I hope for more mystic experiences like the purple circle against the sky. More signs. And Nellie seems to believe in these things too and be plugged into them.

Nellie stomps up the three steps to the trailer door and bangs loudly on it.

A woman trailing scarves and gypsy-type clothes answers. "Madame Crenshaw, your future's in your hands."

"My future is in Jesus's hands," says Nellie.

"You're entitled to your opinion," says Madame Crenshaw.

We go inside. Madame Crenshaw has to make way for Nellie's bulk.

"My next-door neighbor, Mabel, tells me you can see the future. If you can prove you can do this, we'd like to hear about this girl's future."

"Happy to. That will be twenty bucks," says Madame Crenshaw.

"I'd like to do an exchange. I do some energy work myself and I could give you a treatment and you could demonstrate your remarkable gift," says Nellie.

"Well, that would be a demonstration of *your* remarkable gift if you could make me give you a demonstration for free," says Madame Crenshaw, and laughs. "I don't do exchanges. Cash in advance."

"Cash stops the flow of energy," says Nellie.

"But it increases the flow of gin," says Madame Crenshaw, sighing and getting a bottle out of the cupboard over the sink. "You want a drop?" she asks Nellie.

Nellie looks uncertain.

Madame Crenshaw turns to me. "You?"

I shake my head.

"Well, Christ, I do," she says, and pours herself half a tumbler, then drinks about half of that all at once. She sits down and crosses her arms over her chest and says, "Well?"

Nellie goes to her purse and opens it reluctantly. She gets out her wallet. It is stuffed with bills and heavy with coins. I gape. "It's not all mine, some of it is from the collection plate, but, of course, I'm not using *that*. I have to make the deposit tomorrow. This twenty is *mine*," she says, peeling it off and handing it to Madame Crenshaw.

Immediately, as if the twenty has flicked the On

switch of her telepathic mind, Madame Crenshaw stands up in a swirl of purple India cotton and begins incanting things we don't understand.

"In English, please," says Nellie.

"I was getting to that," says Madame Crenshaw irritably. She grabs one of Nellie's hands, sits down, and holds it over her heart, staring into space, her pupils dilating.

I can see that Nellie is about to snatch her hand back when Madame Crenshaw says, "I can feel in your hand you've got great preaching powers." Then Madame Crenshaw takes Nellie's hand off her heart and looks at the palm. Nellie relaxes her hand in Madame Crenshaw's and stares at it as if trying to see what Madame Crenshaw does. "What you don't realize is you've got great healing powers. You ever done any faith healing?"

"You mean like energy work? That's another name for energy work! Isn't it, Jane?" she asks me.

I nod but I'm no expert.

"You are right to do it. You must do it. You're *intended* to do it," says Madame Crenshaw, dropping her hand and looking far far away. "You've got the gift."

The cadence of this reminds me of *Millions of Cats*. Hundreds of cats, thousands of cats, millions and billions and trillions of cats. This runs over and over in my mind and I try to remember the last time I read this story. Why can't I stay focused? I don't want to be skeptical but some tiny part of me is thinking that she isn't telling Nellie anything Nellie hasn't already told *her*. But I am afraid that if I am skeptical, the universe won't reveal things to me. Nellie talks about being open to it all. If you aren't open, maybe these mystical things don't happen to you.

"What gift?" asks Nellie, although it seems obvious to me. I think she just wants to hear it again. Everyone wants to think they're extra-talented.

"*The* gift," says Madame Crenshaw, looking sideways.

"*The* gift?"

"*That's* the one," says Madame Crenshaw, starting to stand up.

"The *healing* gift," breathes Nellie in hushed, awed tones.

"Yeah, it's the holy grail of gifts, all right. Anyone mind if I smoke?"

"My mother always did say I was good with my hands," whispers Nellie. She is turning her hands palm up to stare at them as if their power might be visible. "And I can move energy. But is that different from healing?"

"Oh, it's different," says Madame Crenshaw.

"How different?"

"*Different.*"

Hundreds of cats, thousands of cats, millions and billions and trillions of cats.

"Praise Jesus."

"Praise Jesus, praise Allah, praise the whole lot of 'em," says Madame Crenshaw, who is beginning to slur her words. She goes back to the cabinet where she got the gin and takes out a pack of cigarettes. She lights one and draws in a lungful of smoke. Then she exhales and at the same time she says, "You ever seen a transparent poodle?"

We shake our heads again.

"You're on this earth for a great purpose but to divine it, you must go to Lake Mattawan, where I found a large, [inhale] transparent poodle."

"Like a . . . a standard poodle?" asks Nellie.

"Is it someone's pet?" I ask.

"What are you talking about?" Madame Crenshaw

snaps at us, exhaling. "This poodle is a poodle into the future."

"A transparent *portal?*" I say. It makes more sense but it is vaguely disappointing.

"I hate dogs," says Nellie.

Madame Crenshaw pours herself another glass of gin and downs it as if thinking about matters. We don't say a thing. We don't want to interrupt her while she's on a roll. "There are time and space poodles in a few places on earth. Transporting poodles. This is one. The energy here runs through a sacred meridian. You must realize this is why you have been drawn to this place. Can you feel its sacred energy?"

"I wasn't drawn here so much as I was born here," says Nellie.

"Me too," I say.

"*You* weren't paid for," Madame Crenshaw says, and turns her back on me. "But YOU!" She says this so loudly that Nellie and I both leap to our feet. We are afraid she is about to spontaneously combust or do one of those other things the *National Enquirer* is always warning you about. "You have a great and sacred purpose."

"You've already said that," I point out, hoping to

108 ···· my one hundred adventures

provide a valuable service and thus get back into
the inner circle, but they both give me such a look
I shut up immediately.

"Well, how do I find this poodle?" asks Nellie.

"It's easy. Find the reeds. It's by the seventh reed
as you wade out from shore."

"The seventh reed!" says Nellie.

"That would make a good book title," I say.

They both look at me again.

"Well, heck, come with us, then," says Nellie.
"We'll find out my sacred purpose together. It'll be
a great moment. The combination of my gifts and
yours."

"Yeah, that'd be nifty but I got this wonky ankle," says Madame Crenshaw, suddenly limping
around the trailer. "Injuries at our age take forever
to heal. You find that? Man, I hate getting old."

Nellie starts to advance on her, hands stretched
out toward her ankle, looking a lot like Franken-
stein's monster, and I think Madame Crenshaw and
I are equally startled until it occurs to us that Nellie is just planning on trying out those healing
hands. Madame Crenshaw falls backward over a
chair trying to get away from her.

"You'd better hurry. You must find this poodle and divine your purpose. All will be shown to you. But the poodle is closing soon. It's a limited-time-only-offer poodle. You know, they don't stick around in one place. I mean, after today it could be off to anywhere, Yellowstone, the Grand Tetons, the Smoky Mountains, Lansing," says Madame Crenshaw. "Grand Rapids."

"In Michigan?" says Nellie. I guess it surprises her. Michigan doesn't seem like a portal place.

"Some people say poodles followed Gerald Ford around," says Madame Crenshaw.

"Gerald Ford was a great president," says Nellie, barely breathing now.

"He was swell," says Madame Crenshaw.

"Hurry, have to hurry," Nellie is muttering to herself, her eyes all glazed. She grabs me by the skirt and yanks me toward the door. "We gotta get to Lake Mattawan before it disappears."

"Lake Mattawan? That's way back toward town," I say.

"That's right, Lake Mattawong . . . ," says Madame Crenshaw, hurrying us along.

"Mattawan," I correct.

"Whatever," says Madame Crenshaw. "Leave your purse and shoes with me. I'll lend you some old tennis shoes so you don't get your high heels mucky, and you don't want to leave the purse in the car. Even if you lock it, they're always breaking into cars there."

Madame Crenshaw looks down at Nellie's shoes, which are the same black high heels I have seen her wear to church for years. Her feet flow over the edges like molten lava. Many Sundays I have sat in boredom staring at her legs driven into those shoes wondering if this week it will be Krakatoa. Nellie looks at her shoes and there is a funny expression on her face as if she should have known that this great portal moment was imminent. As if here it is, the moment she knew all her life was coming, the time when someone finally recognizes her greatness and is willing to show her her destiny—and wouldn't you know it, she's wearing the wrong shoes.

Madame Crenshaw goes to a closet and throws Nellie a pair of old tennis shoes. They're a little big but no one is wasting time worrying about that. We have to get to the portal.

"We're imposing on you. Taking your shoes," says Nellie awkwardly, slowing down at the doorway.

"Are you kidding? It's a PORTAL! A PORTAL!" says Madame Crenshaw, only it comes out "A POODLE! A POODLE!" with some smoke in a fit of coughing. She is lighting one cigarette off the next. You'd think the portal would have shown her emphysema or lung cancer and scared a little sense into her.

"Oh, but wait," I say. "What about me and the absolution? The, you know, the *future?*" I say as obliquely as I can to Nellie. "If you can lend me twenty dollars, I promise to pay you back."

"Gotta go, kids," says Madame Crenshaw, trying to shove me out the door. She is in as great a hurry as Nellie.

Nellie says, "Well, maybe just a quick reading, can you hand me my purse?"

"Never mind the purse; it'll be a freebie, okay?" says Madame Crenshaw, kicking Nellie's purse into the closet and snatching up my hand and rattling this off: "You and your best friend are going to be parted soon."

"Because I am going to *jail?*" I squawk.

"NO."

"Because I'm going to *hell?*" I squawk even louder.

"Quit interrupting. No, it's someplace empty with nothing much to see. That's where you're going and now you have to LEAVE or your friend here is going to miss the poodle, move it, move it, move it!" She slams the door behind us.

"Okay. We'll be back soon," calls Nellie, and we scurry off to the car. Nellie has to shuffle to keep the shoes on.

We drive like the dickens back to the lake, park in the lot and lock the doors. We don't have to worry about Nellie's purse but there are all those Bibles inside. I say we were going to give the Bibles away anyhow, why can't people just take them, and Nellie says there's a big difference between giving Bibles away and people stealing them, but I swear she just hasn't thought this through.

"Now where are them weeds?" asks Nellie as we walk along the side of the lake.

"I think she said *reeds,*" I say mildly. I am getting my good shoes dirty but no one seems to care about this. I realize the best thing to do is to take them off and wade barefoot through the lake rather than try to walk along the bushy shore.

"This had better be some poodle," says Nellie as the hem of her dress gets caught on a bush. There is a ripping sound and I think I hear her say a bad word but of course I must be wrong. Nellie thinks what we say affects our energies and she is very careful.

The lake is big and we can't see around the next bend. Nellie is wading through the water now too, still wearing Madame Crenshaw's old tennis shoes. It is taking me longer than her because I am picking my way over rocks and looking for crayfish.

"I hope you don't think I always have truck with stuff like this," Nellie says, her voice drifting back over her shoulder. "Predictions and psychic poodles and such."

"She said *portal*, Nellie," I say.

"Portal, poodle, it's probably all the same. Anyhow, I've got no truck with the occult but there are some Christian goodly sorts, well, the prophets in the Bible, for instance . . ." She says this last so defensively I keep quiet and don't even tell her that the whole thing is a fine adventure as far as I'm concerned. I want to see the psychic poodle too.

We stump along silently for a while.

My dress is wet up to my waist and we still haven't found any reeds. This is a pretty reedless lake, it seems to me.

"You know what I think? I think what she was trying to tell us is that the portal *is* a poodle," says Nellie as we find no reeds or portals.

"WHAT?" I say.

"The portal has to have a shape, don't it? The portal is a poodle. That's why she kept saying 'portal' and we kept hearing 'poodle.' Because it was both, right?"

"Well, then someone has to own it," I say. "And I don't see anyone owning a transporting portal."

"Not if it's wild. Lives in a cave, no doubt."

"A feral poodle?" I ask.

"A poodle portal," corrects Nellie. "Didn't you hear her say how it was traveling on? Can't do that if you're owned by someone. You gotta think about things more, child."

What I'm thinking is that the sun is getting

to her. Either that or she is thinking too hard about this whole thing and her brains are over-heating.

We keep walking in silence except for birdsong. I see the dock where my mother fishes but there is no one there today. In fact, for such a fine summer day there doesn't seem to be anyone at the lake. Then we go around the bend and immediately there's nothing but—canoeists and swimmers and rowboats and people floating in inner tubes. There's a lakeside lodge here, that's why. I've never been to this part of the lake before because it's so far from the public parking lot. Everyone looks rich and kind of snooty and when they see Nellie and me picking our way over rocks and logs through the water they become still. I can feel their rich eyes boring into us. I see what they see suddenly and realize we are like an apparition to them—two people in Sunday dresses, one in nylons and old, slightly too large tennis shoes, stumping along the shallow edge of the lake as fast as they can as if on a mission.

One of the attendants onshore, wearing a white jacket and carrying a drink tray, comes running down and says, "I'm sorry, ma'am, but this part of the lake is for guests only."

"What?" asks Nellie, paying no attention and stumping right past him. I think for a second she is just going to swipe at him waist level with that massive arm of hers and knock him into the water and keep going.

He runs like a little dog at her heels, saying, "You can't go here. You must turn back."

"We're looking for a poodle portal," says Nellie. I can't help feeling this isn't helping our case.

"Well, no dogs are allowed here either," says the waiter as if this settles it.

"We're running out of time," says Nellie. "This portal poodle is going to up and close in on itself any second. We need to count the reeds but we haven't seen any reeds." I am wondering if she has heatstroke or something. She's all sweaty and talking to herself.

"You have to go! NOW!" says the waiter so rudely that I stop being embarrassed. He is not at all concerned for her health even though it is clear Nellie is under some great physical strain. She is not built for this kind of hike. Also, we're in the lake. They can't own the lake or even this part of it. Even I know that.

"You know how far it is to the reeds?" asks Nellie, swinging around to look at him as she realizes he could be useful.

"Madame, I can assure you we are a reed-free facility," says the uppity young man, and now I think I may knock him into the water if Nellie doesn't. But fortunately we have been moving at a good pace during this whole confrontation while the waiter mincingly runs at our heels and in another minute we are around the next bend and into a wild part of the lake again and the waiter, as if there is an invisible fence keeping him back, stays rooted to his side of the bend, calling triumphantly after us, "And don't come back."

I would like to go back and get a little mud on his jacket but if there is a portal, it probably isn't open to people who behave in this way. I'm not sure it's open to people who even *think* in this way.

Nellie mumbles something but I can't tell what. We stump along again in silence around bend after bend, Nellie muttering periodically to herself, and I think I hear snatches of hymns and prayers and wonder if she is exhorting the universe to show itself or just trying to keep her spirits up. Anyhow we have been going a good hour and a half when we find ourselves suddenly looking at an old blue car and we're so tired it takes us a second to realize we're right back in front of the parking lot where we began.

"We missed it," says Nellie, so disheartened that she plops right down where she is, which unfortunately is in six inches of water. "The portal poodle must have closed."

"It might have closed because I had bad thoughts about the waiter," I say. I want Nellie to tell me my energies are really just fine but "I'm afraid you could be right," she says musingly.

We get wetly back into her front seat and she's so bedraggled and confused she doesn't even bother to spread newspapers on the seats to keep them clean. We get lake muck all over them. Her nylons are ripped. Her dress is ripped. There's a twig in her hair. I am soaked up to my armpits and my feet are a mess of tiny bleeding cuts.

"But we didn't even find the reeds. Where were the reeds?" I ask.

"Probably disappeared with the portal poodle when you had those bad thoughts," says Nellie.

We drive silently back to the trailer to tell our sad tale to Madame Crenshaw. I am so tired I am not paying much attention to the road when suddenly Nellie stops the car. She says nothing and at first I don't see why she has halted and then I do. Ahead of us are the tracks where Madame Crenshaw's trailer once stood.

We sit and stare at them for a while. Then we drive back to town. Nellie says nothing. Her mouth never stops working.

Finally she says, "Do you suppose the portal came and got her?"

"No," I say after a long pause.

"You suppose the cops came along and made her move?"

"Maybe," I say, but our sheriff is a pretty sensible sort and I can't really see it if she wasn't hurting anyone. "Anyhow, it doesn't much matter." Then I remember. "She had your purse."

Nellie's mouth keeps working.

"And your shoes."

We both think about this.

"She said I was destined for a great purpose. You heard her, didn't you?"

"Yes," I say slowly. Then for the first time I realize Madame Crenshaw never told me anything about the Gourd baby. And she said I was moving someplace empty with nothing much to see when we have no plans to move at all.

"Maybe she's back in town or coming back tomorrow," says Nellie after a bit.

I think Nellie is a better person than me because she wants to give Madame Crenshaw the benefit of the doubt and I do not. I want to say, She took your *purse* and your *shoes!* But I know that Nellie will just see this as more evidence that I have a closed, unforgiving heart, and maybe she is right.

There is a long silence in the car. In fact, it lasts until we get back to the parking lot by my beach and Nellie stops. She does not say anything and she doesn't look left or right while she parks so it's a good thing there don't happen to be any small children or animals in the way. As I get out I notice that the cigarette man is there again and I start to mention it to Nellie, leaning in the window of the door I have just closed. But she takes off so fast I have to leap back and I watch her car zooming down Main Street until it disappears altogether in a cloud of dust.

When I get halfway down the beach I feel someone's eyes on my back and turn, wondering if Nellie has returned, but there is no one there except the cigarette man and he is not staring at me. He is staring out to sea.

Mr. Fordyce

My Seventh Adventure

Mrs. Gourd explained to Ginny and me that once she starts work we have to be at her trailer at eight a.m. so she can start her first day on the job at the Bluebird Café at nine. It doesn't take an hour for her to walk over there, but she wants some of that time for readying herself in front of the mirror without little D children scurrying around her clean white uniform. She is touchingly proud of that waitress uniform and the little half hat she wears on her head with its print of blue-birds on top. When we arrive, before we can head for the beach, she wants to model it for us. I think maybe she has never belonged to anything before. Once she puts it on, you can see her lifting her head a little higher. She isn't a nobody anymore, she is a *waitress*.

She keeps us in the trailer for a while, asking our opinion about the angle of her hat and whether to leave her top button open or close it. Ginny and I admit to each other that as we watch her, purse slung over her shoulder, jaunty lift to her usually plodding stride, making her way to town to her respectable job, we feel a measure of pride. Her excitement is contagious. It is because of us she can do this thing.

I feel good until I remember that because of me Willie Mae may be permanently damaged.

Mr. Gourd is sacked out on the couch and when Mrs. Gourd leaves, he gets up and takes a beer out of the fridge. He stares at us as we grab the children's sand pails. "GET OUT OF HERE!" he bellows, falling against the kitchen table. Ginny and I scoot out, leaving behind the rest of the toys we meant to gather up. My heart pounds. We take the children, with Darvon sobbing, as far away from the trailer as we can before we even breathe again.

At the beach we settle into sandy boredom. It is going to be a long day.

"I didn't know it would be so hard to watch children," says Ginny. She has just checked her watch. We have been on the beach fifteen minutes.

"No," I say. I don't think Max and Hershel and Maya are this hard to watch but I have never done it all day.

"I'm never having any myself," says Ginny.

"Oh, Ginny, don't babysit with me if it's going to make you feel that way," I say.

"What's so terrible?" asks Ginny. "More people should want not to have children. World over-population is the biggest problem on the planet. I was on the fence about it before, but now I know for sure. I don't want any. They're disgusting."

"Your children won't be. They won't be like the Gourds, for heaven's sake," I say. I look at the little Gourd baby in his carrier. We take the liberty of removing the blanket Mrs. Gourd always keeps draped over it. He blinks in the unaccustomed light. He probably just needs some stimulation.

"They may not be like the Gourds, they may be delightful, but it is clear to me that they wear you down. And I don't want to be worn down. I want to design fabulous clothes for horrible women dripping in wealth who can afford them and who will invite me to their silly, pretentious parties."

Ginny's ambitions never make a lot of sense to me but they somehow keep a fire burning in her that propels her forward every day. Mrs. Gourd always looked fireless but now with this new job she begins to look different, as if she is being propelled forward too. A fire is starting to burn in her as well. I think this fire changes everything about a person. Now she won't look tired all the time. Now maybe we are going to be the ones who look tired all the time. Me, because my one hundred adventures must be put on hold. I cannot have such adventures with so many people in tow. I long to venture forth alone. I am suffocating, my fires of purpose dwindling to embers. I tell Ginny all this while we sit on the beach, and she stares at me the whole time, her mouth slightly open, her eyes round and fathomless, but she says nothing.

The morning drifts on; we make sand angels and talk and help the children with their castles and occasionally pass out snacks. We have taken a jar of peanut butter and some bread from the Gourd cabinet to avoid having to go back and face Mr. Gourd in his undershirted glory.

It really isn't so bad, only another four hours of this, I think, when a car pulls up to the public lot. Cigarette Guy is already there sitting on a cement divider and watching the waves crash. He hasn't started smoking yet. He eyes the car with curiosity and then Ginny sees it and says, "What's my mom doing here?"

But she doesn't go up to greet her. Instead Mrs. Cavenaugh walks down to the beach looking primly annoyed. She takes a starfish out of one of the Gourds' mouth. A little something we have missed but when you're watching five children at once you do tend to miss things from time to time.

"These children are filthy," she says.

"Well, we aren't paid to give them baths," says Ginny. "In fact, we aren't paid at all."

"Anyhow, tell your little friend goodbye," says Mrs. Cavenaugh. Mrs. Cavenaugh always refers to me as Ginny's little friend, I think because she secretly hopes I will shrink to nothingness and disappear altogether. It is extremely wishful and imaginative thinking on Mrs. Cavenaugh's part. "Come on, we have to go. I have enrolled you in soccer camp."

Mrs. Cavenaugh grabs Ginny by the upper arm and hauls her to her feet. This surprises me. Ginny seems surprised by it too.

"Ouch," she says, yanking her arm free. We've been taught at school how to deal with potential kidnappers. Always make a fuss and resist. I wait patiently for Ginny to start screaming "NO, NO, NO," which is step one, but she doesn't.

"But I thought soccer camp was full," says Ginny.

"There was a cancellation. I had you on a waiting list."

"And you told me I didn't have to go to any more camps this summer. That I could stay home and design dresses."

"Are you designing dresses right now? Besides, I don't recall saying anything of the sort," says Mrs. Cavenaugh.

"But you did," says Ginny.

"Well, if I did then it was so you could design dresses, and you have broken your end of the bargain. Now, don't make a fuss. Think of the example you are setting for the little Gourds."

The little Gourds care so much that they don't even notice Ginny leaving, but I watch her dispirited trudge behind her mother through the sand back to their car with mounting terror. Now I have four hours alone with the five of them and no one at all to talk to. I will go stark staring mad. I begin to understand Mrs. Gourd better and better. Also the thrill of working at the Bluebird Café.

Ginny doesn't even turn around to say goodbye. I wonder if she feels guilty because she is secretly relieved to be hauled off like this. To be forced into something that either of us would consider paradise next to Gourd-sitting.

I am sorry to say that by noon, after countless trips to the public washroom with all five Gourds, because I don't dare leave any of them on the beach, these little excursions being the height of excitement after long minutes of watching sand blow across the horizon and watching the Gourds, who are getting restless, slap each other with whatever is handy, I begin to understand even Mr. Gourd's method of dealing with tedium. It is then that I decide I will take the Gourds on a long trek. It will be like the Long March. History always seems to be full of downtrodden people being forced to march great distances for other people's convenience and if it works for those dictators it should work for me. At worst it will tire out the little Gourds and I can't help feeling that if we lose a few on the wayside the senior Gourds will be extremely forgiving. So we start to trek.

"Where are we going?" asks Dean, who, being one of the brighter Gourds, has noticed that we are changing our location.

"Well, now, if I told you it wouldn't be a surprise, would it?" I say.

We go down Main Street and when they see we are not stopping at the drugstore for penny candy or the Dairy Queen or even (I consider their upbringing) one of the taverns, they begin to squawk. They cannot imagine good things beyond these borders.

"Think of the cathedral at Pisa," I say. "Covent Garden. Café life in Paris." I am not familiar with any of these things exactly but at least I have heard of them. I hope to spark something within.

"I don't want to walk no more," says Darvon.

"Any. Anymore," I say. I decide that the best way to deal with their protests is never to address them directly but to use them as an opportunity for grammar lessons.

"I don't want to go no more," says Dee Dee, sitting down determinedly on the sidewalk.

"Anymore, anymore, Dee Dee, " I say. "Look, there is an especially pretty sight at the end of this hike. Like a pot of gold at the end of the rainbow."

"What pot of gold?"

"What's a pot of gold?"

"I don't want to go no more."

"I'm hungry."

"Darvon ate a rock."

"You should put a blanket on Willie Mae's head."

"I don't like Willie Mae. He cries."

This seems the most extraordinary statement, because Willie Mae has not cried once all day. I put it down to the stimulation of life without the blanket. Willie Mae is seeing the world for once. Willie Mae may have prayed for a hundred adventures himself, for all I know, and I am facilitating them for him. I wonder if he cried a lot more prior to being beaned with a Bible and then am so full of guilt that I let the children rest five minutes before I make them start walking again.

They are better about it than I thought they would be. They trudge on without any questions about where we are going. My feet are sore, my own brain is nearly dead. I didn't want any of the Gourds' grimy peanut butter or bread so I am starving and I still have two and a half hours to kill. We stop now and then on our trek across town, sometimes on curbs to watch children who own toys and bikes and things playing sensible games. We stop in at the school playground until I see that it is dangerous. I can't keep the four of them from breaking their necks all at once. Darvon runs up the slide. Dee Dee hangs on the teeter-totter and gets a splinter. I tell her we will show it to her mother later because I have nothing to remove it with. This makes her scream and cry. It is time to get walking again.

And then finally we are on the other side of town, right at the edge, and here the town stops as if someone has drawn it along a line, and beyond is just blank paper. I wonder what it will be like to leave the sidewalk and go into the blankness. As we continue on, I imagine we are going into the twilight zone. Then I think, I am walking endlessly with four children and a baby, I *am* in the twilight zone. We head toward a small copse of trees and a road winding into meadows.

"Where's the gold?" asks Darvon. I have forgotten all about that.

That's when I spy the trailer on the other side of the copse of trees. It is a different style from the Gourds' or Madame Crenshaw's garish purple one. This one is silver and bullet shaped. There is a card table set up on the grass next to it with chairs around it. The trailer has flower boxes in the windows so I know it is permanent. I begin to see that on the outskirts of our town there live a whole subset of people, all in trailers. As if these people have chosen to put themselves apart from the community. Not belonging but not wholly adrift either, the way barnacles can attach to sea turtles, not turtle but living nonetheless, organically connected. I suppose Ginny's mother may see my mother that way but we are not trailer people. I don't know what makes us different. It is more as if my mother is a light that the town would attach to if it could. But you cannot attach to light, it is amorphous, you can only be in it.

"Where's the gold?" asks Darvon again.

"There," I say, thoughtlessly because I am ruminating about these things, and I point at the silver trailer and then am immediately sorry because all four Ds run madly for it even though I don't think any of them really cares about a pot of gold. I sigh. I will have to round them up before they trespass on the owner. However, I now know that all I need to do to get them out from underfoot is to point randomly in some direction and say "There." I consider passing on this helpful tip to Mrs. Gourd but decide she's too much of a stinker.

The door to the trailer opens and all four Ds are struck dumb, which is a startling event in itself. Then I see why. Santa Claus has emerged. But it is not Santa, it is a short, fat man with lots of fluffy white hair and a long white beard, wearing a red T-shirt. He opens his mouth but there are no ho ho ho's. You'd think someone who looked like that would feel oddly compelled. Instead he says, "That's an awful lot of kids to babysit."

I don't know how he knows I am babysitting and am not a Gourd myself and then in horror realize that maybe he thinks I am the Gourds' older sibling babysitter, and I am about to set the record straight when Willie Mae begins to cry for the first time all day. I reach into the diaper bag for the bottle. The children scramble around the card table, which has a bowl of raspberries on it. They don't even ask but just dig in. The man turns and goes into the trailer while I put a bottle in Willie Mae's mouth.

"Don't eat those raspberries, they aren't yours," I hiss at the children, who ignore me.

The man comes back out with a big box of toys, which he puts down by the trailer steps. Darvon spies it first and the four of them descend on it with whoops of joy. I don't even bother telling them that it's rude not to ask because the man has clearly brought it out to get them out of his raspberries. He takes the empty raspberry bowl and goes back into the trailer. Then he comes out with a fresh bowl of raspberries, a pitcher of lemonade and two glasses. He invites me to sit down so I sit and continue giving Willie Mae his bottle. I don't know what to say. I am so grateful for this kindness. I remember all those Bible stories of people being offered water at wells and whereas I used to think, Big deal, water, now I understand the

inexplicable warmth you receive from being offered a chair and a cold drink. I have never been
footsore and thirsty and lone enough to appreciate
it before.

I am shy. The man doesn't seem discombobu-
lated at all. He nods toward the toy box and says,
"I have grandchildren. They don't live around here
but I like to keep it for when they visit."

I still don't know what to say. So we just sit there
quietly for a long time and I ask him finally about
his children. He has two and they live in Florida
but they come up for visits with the grandchildren,
of which there are seven. Also, he says he has had
several children by different women and that it is
a strange thing, not the way he would have expected his life to turn out, but he offers no more
information about it so I don't say anything more
and neither does he and I think how maybe he
never talks to anyone, sitting here hour after hour
eating berries, and so such a strange and personal
fact comes spilling out because people need to tell
people things, and then as if to break an awkward
silence he says, "Have you ever read Robert Frost?"

I shake my head.

"He's a poet."

"I know," I say. "My mother is a poet."

"What's her name?" asks the man.

"Felicity Fielding," I say.

"Oh!" he says, startled, and he stares at me hard and then takes two long gulps of lemonade. Finally he gets up and goes back into the trailer. He returns with some books. The one on top is *Snow*. The book that my mother won the Pulitzer for.

"I like your mother's poetry," he says. "I think she's very good. I like Robert Frost too. Who should we read?"

"Well, I know my mother's poetry. Some of it," I say. I don't tell him that I don't really like to hear my mother's poetry. It is as if she becomes someone else and is not my mother. It is mostly just embarrassing. I don't want to know her private thoughts. I mean her very private thoughts. I like to think she is thinking of our feelings the way she always seems to, not that she is having feelings of her own.

"All right, then, let me get some more raspberries." He goes inside and I leaf through the Robert Frost book and then pick up my mother's. Inside she has written, "To Anton Fordyce. For you, dear Anton. For lovely evenings and with gratitude for finding Mrs. Martin!" He is Anton but who is Mrs. Martin? The name rings a bell and then it comes back. Mrs. Martin used to babysit us. My mother would put me to bed and say "Mrs. Martin is coming for a few hours tonight." This is why I never saw any boyfriends, because my mother didn't bring them home. Instead, Mrs. Martin came. And perhaps there were other babysitters before her that I was too young to notice or remember.

My thoughts are interrupted when Mr. Fordyce brings out a bowl of berries for the Gourd children, which they ignore. They are into the toys now and have very limited attention. He puts another bowl of berries on the table for us.

Then without further ado he picks up the Robert Frost book and turns its dignified, old, thin pages, the crackling sound somehow becoming part of the poetry, and reads. When he gets to the lines that go "I am overtired / Of the great harvest I myself desired," I think, This guy is really good.

It is such a luxury to be read to. Not to have to make a response or remember any of it and keep

my attention focused. Sometimes my mind wanders to Mrs. Martin. Is this when my mother would
meet the clothes hanger man? I am sad to give up
my myths, the things I have secretly believed since
I was little, that I was conceived in the depths of a
moonlit sea by tides and eddies and swirls of sea
life and the longing of a poet to be a mother.

And yet, I think, even if the reality is somewhat
more mundane, this too can be true. All our lives
are mundane but all our lives are also poetry.

Whether my mind wanders around these thoughts
or I am caught up by a line Mr. Fordyce reads and
my mind is trailing after the rest of the poem, it is
all okay. It is an afternoon of the greatest charity,
this reading in the shade on a warm day with the
words I can listen to or not as I like, with the berries available and lemonade to take as I will. I can
feel my feet, which were tired, moist and swollen
when I sat down, shrinking back to their bony
normal size, able to wriggle around freely in my
shoes again. Willie Mae has stopped crying and I
put him in his baby carrier, where he goes to sleep.
I lean back in my chair. There are tons of birds in
the big oak tree that is sheltering us. They are
singing quietly. What are all these birds doing in

this tree? The children are playing happily with the new toys. We go on this way for an hour and the man never lifts his eyes from the pages. Then he reads, "Nothing Gold Can Stay," and I say it myself, Nothing gold can stay, nothing gold can stay, and look at my watch and realize it is true because I have to take the children home now.

"I have to go," I say, standing up.

"Please tell your mother hello," says the man.

"My name is Jane Fielding," I say. "These children are the Gourds." It seems too much to list their names.

"My name is Anton Fordyce," says the man, but all our names seem superfluous. He does not stand up but he puts the book down.

"Thanks for the raspberries and the lemonade," I say.

He nods. I make the children put the toys back in the box and we leave the blankness and past the sharp edges of houses, are swallowed into town. I turn one last time to glance at Mr. Fordyce. I almost expect him to have disappeared but he can just be glimpsed beyond the trees, reading quietly and eating raspberries.

Mabel's Cousin the Channeler

My Eighth Adventure

The Blueberries Are Ripe

"Jane," says my mother as I start out the door. I am on my way to care for the little Gourds as I have for the last two weeks except on the weekend, when I see Ginny and deliver Bibles. Ginny's mother has put her in soccer camp right until school starts. Ginny feels bad that she can't help me and is very upset with her mother, who doesn't seem to care that camp is making Ginny miserable. That Ginny counted on her summer to work on her dress designs. Now at the end of her day she is too tired to be creative. She says she feels like a steam kettle with a plugged hole. Any moment she will pop.

I want to tell my mother all this but of course I

cannot. She must wonder that I am never, ever at home this summer but I can tell her nothing. I never told her that Mr. Fordyce said hello. How could I explain my afternoon there? And as the days slip by and I have not told her where I go, I have become more deeply mired in a kind of secrecy that sets me apart from her and Hershel and Maya and Max. I am not here when Max sees whales.

My mother does not look at me. She says, "Jane, could you stay home and watch Maya and Max and Hershel for me today? Henry has asked me to go antiquing with him."

I don't know how much she sees H. K. Thomson when I am not around. I never would have thought my mother would have an interest in someone like him. I feel that just as I have a secret life, my mother is not someone that I knew as well as I thought. It is as if we are losing each other, and a deep sadness fills me. Nothing gold can stay. This is the first time she has asked me to watch Max and Maya and Hershel since I started my adventures, but of course I can't.

When I say no with no explanation she looks concerned. "I know you're busy these days . . . ," she says, and lets it hang there. I can't explain and am aware how surly it makes me appear. She is making jam with the blueberries she and Max and Hershel and Maya picked together yesterday. I love blueberry picking. I love the bogs and the discovery of always more berries clustered together. I hate the bees. I am frequently stung picking blueberries but it is worth it. I look at the big pots of blueberries on the kitchen table and our pantry filling with another row of jam jars and I am sad. It is as if I am missing summer. It is as if I am missing my life. It is happening here without me.

"That's okay," says my mother, seeing my face. "Run along."

I run out and the dark green screen door bangs behind me. It makes a whomping sound. It is one of my favorite sounds in the world. It is the sound of the house breathing. The screen door is its lungs. We keep the house breathing through our movement. What keeps *us* breathing through its movement? The house is the sixth member of the family. The one that is always watching. Under its roof, we are one.

I see H.K. trudging down the beach toward our

house. His head is at a strange angle. H.K. always looks like he's walking into the wind.

I hurry down the beach. It is a cool, damp morning and I pull the corners of my cardigan closer to my body. As H.K. passes he gives me a sickly smile. Not because he wants to smile at me, but because he thinks he has to. I drop my head and move along faster.

Mrs. Gourd has got the little Gourds herded in the front yard, if you can call it that. She has a cardigan on too. Hers is pulled tightly in as well. We are all reining ourselves in this morning. She has a patent leather pocket book over her forearm. It looks shiny and new. I wonder if she has spent her tips on it. I wonder why they are all waiting in the yard like that and then I hear it. Pans and pots being thrown around inside like some great beast is floundering around in his cage. Shouted oaths. Mostly about how he is going to kill Mrs. Gourd.

"Take the children down to the beach. For the whole day. Do you hear me?" she whispers savagely in my ear. "And do not bring them back. I will come for them down there after work."

I do not know what to say. I have never heard

sounds like that before. They frighten me. I take the children quickly away but know I cannot take them to the beach. I cannot be seen today by my mother. I have told her that I cannot take Hershel and Max and Maya. Even if I explain to her that I am babysitting the Gourds, without telling her why, it will not explain why I couldn't also take Hershel and Maya and Max. That I am afraid the Gourd children will tell about Willie Mae and the dropped Bible. That Maya will then blurt it out to my mother. Even if I tell her not to. Small children cannot keep secrets. I am surprised my mother has not seen us before and decide the beach is no longer an option. But where?

I am on Main Street, walking up and down contemplating a destination, and have just decided to visit Mr. Fordyce when I am accosted by Nellie Phipps, who has come out of the hardware store carrying paint cans. She tries to hang on to my arm but misses and grabs me by the collarbone, something I did not know up until this moment was possible.

"Wait up just a minute there, child." She sees the Gourds around my knees and says, "What are all *these?*"

"They're Gourds, of course," I say. Then I hope

she knows that this is their last name and I am not being sarcastic.

"Gourds, are they? They're very small Gourds. Very messy Gourds."

They all still have peanut butter and jelly smeared around their faces from breakfast but you cannot blame Mrs. Gourd this time. She had to get them out in a hurry.

"Yes," I begin, but Nellie cuts me off. "Bring them along."

"Bring them along where?" I ask. I have remembered now that I told her about the Gourd baby. I hope Nellie isn't going to suggest trying out her faith healing on him. We do not know yet what she can actually do. She could experiment and make things worse.

"I am having my house painted so I am going over to Mabel's to get away from the fumes. Her cousin is visiting. She channels."

I wonder if this has something to do with televisions but am so busy keeping the Gourd children on track through town that I don't ask.

Nellie drops off the paint at her house and then we go to Mabel's.

Mabel is even fatter than Nellie. She wears a

large, shapeless short-sleeved flowered dress with snaps up the front. I wonder if it is a dress or a bathrobe. She has on matted pink used-to-be-fluffy slippers and has large dark circles under her eyes. She doesn't look healthy. When she opens the door she just stares at us, not even saying hello. Nellie says, "Move out of the way, Mabel, and ask us in. This is Jane, who dropped the Bible on the baby, scarring it for life. Remember I told you about that?"

"Nellie!" I say, too distraught to remember to call her Miss Phipps. But then I realize I don't really need to worry about Mabel knowing because she just shakes her head like she is trying to get water out of her ear and steps out of the way. I'm not even sure she has taken in what Nellie has said.

Inside there is a woman wearing a long white embroidered caftan.

The children start racing around the house until Nellie yells, "STOP THAT!" and gives them an entire bag of plastic cups, and forks and spoons to play with. This makes them very happy.

We go into the backyard. I check to be sure it is

completely fenced in. I do not want to lose a bunch of Gourds so early in the day. The Gourds start digging with their plastic spoons, filling their plastic cups. It is a worthwhile pursuit and we leave them to it.

When Nellie and I are seated again Mabel's cousin looks at me and says to Nellie, "Is she here for a session too?"

"She's here to watch," says Nellie.

"Watch what?" I ask.

"I told you. She channels," says Nellie. "Spirits use her to speak to us."

"From the beyond," says Mabel's cousin.

"Beyond what?" I ask.

"These mortal shores," says the channeler, yawning as if she has answered all these questions before. Then she explains that yawning means she is beginning to leave her body because the spirits are anxious to communicate. She asks Mabel to light some candles.

We sit in the dim light with the blinds all drawn. It is very eerie. The channeler closes her eyes and makes noises like she is eating something particularly enjoyable. When she opens her eyes finally and says, "Greetings," it is not her own voice. That is, it is her voice but as if she is now an old lady. "How can I help you, my dear, dear Nellie?"

"Well, I'll be ding-donged," whispers Nellie.

"Is she a ghost?" I whisper to Nellie.

"Shhh," says Nellie. "You'll scare it away."

I close my mouth immediately, lean back and fall off my chair. I am afraid *that* may scare the entity away but it chuckles. Apparently nothing fazes it.

"Ding-dong! Ha, ha. Yes, you are fond of that expression. An amusing expression. Such amusing expressions you have on this plane," says the voice.

"Does she think we're in an airplane?" I ask. "Shouldn't we tell her?"

"She means earthly plane," says Mabel, speaking for the first time.

Of course.

"Ask, my child," says the voice to Nellie.

"Who are you?" asks Nellie.

"A spirit. An entity, perhaps you would call me. I cannot give you a name because here in the ether we have many names. But you have questions, I perceive."

"My hands," says Nellie tentatively. You can tell

she isn't quite sure about this whole thing either. It seems so unlikely.

"Ah yes, your gift," says the entity.

"That's what Madame Crenshaw called it, isn't it?" says Nellie, poking me in the ribs.

Yes, I think, but was Madame Crenshaw really clairvoyant? The purse and shoes never showed up again. Stay open, I admonish myself. You cannot see miracles if you are not open to them.

"Of course," the entity says smoothly. "You seek to hide your gift but we see it."

"It's not that I'm hiding it," says Nellie, who is getting agitated, I can tell, "so much as I can't ding-dong figure out how it works."

"How it works?" says the entity. "But you move energy, my child, you know this."

"I mean the healing part," says Nellie.

"Oh, that," says the entity. I don't think it sounds very entity-like but it quickly recovers its savoir-faire and says, "That wondrous part. Yes, my child, you have that. In spades."

It seems to me that the entity goes in and out locution-wise but that is only my opinion and what do I know of entities?

"I feel my time fading," says the entity, and its voice is becoming weak and scratchy. "But you must know you have a great destiny. I see gatherings and you and your child giving many healing sessions."

"My child?" says Nellie.

"Her child?" I say. I can't help myself.

"She ain't got a child," says Mabel.

This seems to confuse the entity. "I mean your soul child. This girl," says the entity, looking at me, although the channeler's eyes are closed so technically I don't know if you can call it looking.

"My soul child?" asks Nellie. Now we are definitely in weird territory and I'm not sure I want to be here.

"Yes. The two of you have had many lives together. You have been twins in a former life. Compadres. Helpmeets. She is on earth to help you heal others. Many will gather for this purpose. The two of you are of the greatly evolved few now living on this planet. It is your destiny to bring others along."

"I'm greatly evolved?" I ask.

"Shhh," says Nellie. "I know what she means."

The entity nods at me. "You have had many

lives. You are a very old soul, my dear, brought
into this lifetime to do great work. There are many
new souls here in this generation. It is your destiny
to help your friend to bring them along. This is
why you are together. Soon the gatherings will
begin."

"Where? When?" asks Nellie.

"I must leave. Bless you, my children," says the
entity. Then the channeler starts to stretch and yawn
again and finally opens her eyes. "Where am I?"
she asks, but Nellie has no use for Mabel's cousin,
who is now just thought of as an entity vehicle.

"Gatherings! People will gather for my healing
hands!" Nellie says. "You'll have to stick close, did
you hear, Jane? In some way you are meant to
help."

"But I thought my energies were blocked or something," I said. Before, Nellie was saying I was in the
spiritual soup, and now she believes I'm evolved.

"I think helping me do this great work is what
will make you evolve further," says Nellie thoughtfully.

"What happened?" asks the channeler, stretch-
ing and blinking.

"Never mind. I gotta go," says Nellie. "I'm going to read up on this channeling stuff on one of the computers at the library."

"That will be fifty dollars," says the channeler, suddenly coming fully awake.

"Fifty dollars!" I say.

But Nellie opens her new purse and pays her. We get the little Gourds out of the backyard. Nellie tells them they can keep the plastic cups and spoons, which I think is kind of rude because they are Mabel's, but Mabel doesn't object. When I thank her for the cups she says she is making potato salad for dinner. The channeler says that's nice, what kind? She is certainly back on planet Earth now. Then she says she is in town for another week on vacation and not doing any more channeling. "It really takes it out of you," she says to me.

"I bet," I say. I don't know what else to say. I have had no practice making chitchat about the trials of giving your body up for a good haunting.

I ask Nellie if the Gourds can play in her backyard until it's time to take them home and at first I think she is going to say no but she just shakes her head suddenly and says, "Did you notice how they *both* talked about my great destiny, Madame Crenshaw and now the spirit? That's how we know this is for real. Because how else would they know this?"

"I wonder where these gatherings are going to be, because your backyard isn't very big, Miss Phipps. Do you think they'll be big gatherings?"

"Oh, BIG!" says Nellie.

"Really big?"

"Huge."

"Then we'd better find you someplace to have them." I am happy to help Nellie with all this if it will make up for dropping the Bible on Willie Mae. And also, if she can do this great thing, it will be so exciting to watch.

"I wonder if the balloonists would let me use their field," says Nellie ruminatively.

"I wouldn't count on it," I say, yawning. If I were a channeler it would mean that the spirits were about to take me over, but no, I'm just tired.

Nellie trots off to the library and the Gourds and I go into Nellie's backyard to make mud pies. It is such a soothing thing to do after all the worry and weight of responsibility. Suddenly all I want is to sit here in the mud spooning twigs into the cups with the Gourds. There are saltwater swans over-head making their way to the sea, their long necks thrust forward. They always look too large and ungainly to fly so that seeing them you gasp a little at all the things you would not guess could be but are anyway. I wish I could follow them down to the sea.

I have been thinking so hard lately that it has been days since I noticed the birds. Now I watch a heron on its way from one pond to another, I sup-pose, and as I follow it an eagle flies by. I used to believe that if I saw an eagle, what I was thinking at that moment must be true. I am endlessly point-ing out birds to Ginny, who accuses me of being a birder, but it still gives me a small gasp of pleasure to see one unexpectedly appear. As if all the move-ment in the universe is visible to us suddenly in the fields of the air.

When Nellie comes back later she says that she has read about channeling and she thinks there might be something to it. A lot of people in Holly-wood endorse it. She thinks we must beg for another session. We head next door. As we walk over I notice Nellie's watch and in horror I see the time. I was supposed to deliver the Gourds to their mother on the beach half an hour ago. I tell Nellie we have to go.

"We need clearer directions about these gatherings. I got questions. I want to know if I should take you in and apprentice you in the art of healing if you're going to be part of this great thing," says Nellie, ignoring me.

"I don't see how that would work with school and babysitting and everything else," I say.

"You heard her, we're soul mates. We need to go back and ask about the particulars."

"Nellie, I CAN'T," I shout. "I've got to meet Mrs. Gourd on the beach or she's going to think . . . I don't know what she's going to think!"

We skeddaddle out of there and then we have to return because I realize we are missing Darsie. I run around and around Nellie's yard, more and more frantic. Luckily we find Darsie under a bush. "Didn't you hear me CALLING?" I yell at her.

"I knew where I was," says Darsie with impeccable logic.

"We have to hurry back to Mommy, hurry back to Mommy," I keep repeating as I take baby running steps, trying to put speed into their little legs because I am afraid Nellie will stop us again and I'll lose the Gourds. I'm exhausted and worried and frantic. Thoughts of the birds are long gone. But I am able to move the little Gourds along. They move unthinkingly like herd animals but despite our speed, when we get to the parking lot Mrs. Gourd is already there, looking furious. She is sitting on the cement divider bumming smokes off the cigarette man and when she sees us she rises like a towering fury and grabs the baby carrier out of my hands, but this is not what captures my attention, for at that moment I hear my mother's voice coming loudly across the sand, shrieking, "NED!" And the cigarette man is off the divider and running down the beach to meet her.

Med

My Ninth Adventure

My mother hugs the cigarette man. He hugs her back. I stare at them thinking he must reek of cigarette smoke and how unpleasant for my mother but even at a distance I can tell she doesn't care. By the time she is done hugging the cigarette man, Mrs. Gourd and all the little Gourds can only be glimpsed swiftly shuffling down Main Street. She can get those children to walk even faster than I can without saying a word.

I was vaguely aware that Mrs. Gourd was haranguing me through the long hug but I did not hear her. I realize I have never seen my mother hug anyone except my brothers and sister and me. Is this man related to her in some way?

And then as they join me it becomes apparent how. He is another one of *them*. One of the men she met when Mrs. Martin came over. I wonder how many more are coming. I wonder if he has fathered one of us. I realize now that when my mother said as she took laundry off the line that the clothes hanger man was "your father" she might have meant any of us children; we were all swarming about at the time and she wasn't specific. If that is right and another father is H.K. and yet another Mr. Fordyce, who really seems too old to me, it is possible that we each of us have a different father and like the *Niña*, the *Pinta* and the *Santa Maria* coming to shore, all the ships are sailing back to port this summer. Things come in waves or come in on tides, the moon pulling our destinies from shore to shore so that what we think is coincidence seldom is.

I eye this cigarette man slit-eyed as he approaches. What does he want? Why sit on cement dividers and stare at the sea?

He holds out his hand to me. "Well, I'll be. I'll be. I'll be. I had no idea. No idea looking at you coming and going that *you* were one of Felicity's daughters."

"Well, I am," I say.

"Well, I'll just be," he says.

"Oh, you've *said* that, Ned," says my mother, laughing. She gives him a small punch on his upper arm and he swings her around in a circle so her feet don't even touch the sand. She is barefoot.

"I have left the others on the beach over by the house. You must come, you must come. And you must *stay*. You can sleep on the couch."

"I don't want to be any trouble," says Ned.

"Oh, you won't be," says my mother. "Will he, Jane?"

"Well, he might be," I say honestly before I think.

"Why didn't you tell me you were here, staying at the Dragonfly Inn and eating at that awful Bluebird Café?" My mother says this quickly to cover up what I have said. They are both pretending not to have heard it but we all have. My face is burning.

"I guess I was afraid of finding out you weren't here. You know, a lot can change after so much time." He gets his backpack out of the trunk of his car with that Ontario license plate.

"Well, that's true," says my mother, in tones that are practically singing. "Come on." She leads him down the beach. I follow at a short distance, which seems to be okay with them. They don't encourage me to keep up. Probably they are worried I am going to say something without thinking again.

Ned seems delighted to meet Hershel and Max especially. I think he likes boys better than girls. I grab Maya's hand and start to walk home with her. I don't hear what Ned says but I hear my mother, who is picking up shovels and pails and putting them into a large beach bag, say, "Well, that will be a treat. All right, see you soon." She and the boys catch up to me and Maya.

"Ned is going into town for some steaks and a bottle of wine and *cupcakes.* Isn't that dear? He thought we should have cupcakes."

"Yum," I say. I am trying not to sound sour but it is tough going. "Why were you going to the parking lot barefoot?" I ask her.

"I thought I saw you there from where we were on the beach. You've been gone so much. I came to greet you. Suddenly I missed you."

I put my arm around my mother's waist and we walk back the rest of the way like this.

While Ned is gone my mother makes a big salad

and rice and she gets a fire going in a circle of stones on the beach. I sit with Maya and Hershel and Max on the low front step of our porch, which goes right into the sand and faces the ocean.

"Whales!" says Max, getting up and pointing.

I don't even look, I just say, "There are no whales, Max."

"Whales!" he says again five minutes later. He must be tired of his LEGOS. He is losing half of them in the sand. "Stop saying that," I say, digging up his LEGOS for him and depositing them at his feet. I feel like a dog.

Maya goes in the house and gets her Sears, Roebuck paper dolls.

"I need more clothes," she says, handing me the scissors and the catalogue.

"You don't need me for this. You know how to cut things out with scissors," I say to her.

"I hate cutting," she says, shoving the catalogue at me. I am really getting tired of little children and the mysterious workings of adults. I wish Ginny were here. I let Maya put the catalogue on my lap but stay slumped over it, my elbows on my knees, staring out to sea.

"You're pensive," says my mother in that jolly voice as she comes in to get more stuff to put on our picnic table. But she sounds a little worried too. She already has plates and napkins and silverware there. Now she is bringing out jam and bread and things we don't normally have with dinner. She puts out strawberry, raspberry and a jar of the new blueberry. She is a jam show-off, I think.

"Well," I begin, but then my mother looks up over my head down the beach and waves her arms wildly over her head. Ned is coming toward the house.

"Greetings," says Ned. He has a plaid mackinaw over his arm, which he dumps on the porch steps like he lives here. He holds up a grill he has in one hand. "I didn't know if you had one."

"That's wonderful. We don't. I wondered after you left how we were going to do this," says my mother.

He also has a bottle of orange pop for us. He pours wine for my mother and himself and pop for all of us. He has bought steaks and cupcakes and a bag of candy and two bags of potato chips and potato salad from the café. My mother says,

"Uh-oh, the Bluebird Café?" She takes a tiny nibble with a fork and says, "You shouldn't have." He takes one off the same fork and says, "You're right, I shouldn't have." They grin. She lets us eat potato chips all over the beach while they sit on the steps and drink wine and heat the grill. Max keeps going up behind Ned and eating potato chips over Ned's head. He is getting a lot of little pieces of chips in Ned's hair. Ned hasn't even reached his hand up to brush them out. Perhaps he cannot feel them because his head is made of stone.

"WHALES!" Max keeps saying to Ned. "Whales!" and pointing out to sea until Ned finally puts his wine down and sweeps Max up like an airplane and runs all over the beach with him. Max screams in delight. My mother laughs. I pour more orange pop moodily into my cup and think about murder-suicides and wonder if they begin with too much food and fun and games. With happy cries echoing over the beach and chip bags blowing in the wind and attacking seagulls and no one paying attention really to the evil thoughts of one person in the group. I know I am wallowing and it is good. Somehow, unlike not praying for Mrs. Nasters, it does not seem like something that will send me to hell. I know part of my problem is that I am tired. It has been such a long workweek with the little Gourds. They have taken every ounce of my energy and I feel it has all been outgoing and nothing has been incoming.

Thinking of the horrible chain of events that has led me to babysitting, I rise to my feet. Why have I not thought of this before? If not praying for Mrs. Nasters and only praying for Mrs. Parks has led to this pass, why can I not reverse the process just as easily? Why can't I pray for Mrs. Nasters and not pray for Mrs. Parks? I have been pacing in a circle in front of the porch steps and am so startled by the elegance of this solution that I trip over a step and land on my knees, spilling pop everywhere.

Ned glances over and says I look like the pilgrims going up the steps of St. Joseph's Oratory in Montreal. Then he tells us about Brother Andre and his miraculous healings and all the crutches hanging in the oratory from lame people who have walked after contact with him.

My mother comes up to me and says, as if imparting some great secret, "Ned is a *Canadian*."

I rise to my feet and say that I have simply tripped.

Ned goes on telling me about Brother Andre's pickled heart. How college boys once stole it out of the oratory as a prank.

All the time Ned is telling this story he is putting the steaks on the grill and through dinner he tells us more.

"Up in New Brunswick is a place where the Vikings landed. They had a whole community there. People have gone to dig up all their tools and stuff. Really made kind of a shambles of the place. The way I look at it, if the Vikings were in this one place then they were probably here and there and around, you know? So I make it my mission, in between odd jobs, to find myself a piece of Viking remains and auction it off on eBay for a fortune."

"Could you do that, Ned?" asks my mother. "Wouldn't the government legally be entitled to it?"

"Well, now, I didn't think of that at the time, but just let me finish the story, Felicity," says Ned. "I was digging every chance I got. Of course, only at night, because, you know, I didn't know where I was going to find a Viking remain. I kept close to the excavation site but I couldn't dig right on that land. It was an archaeological site, after all. A Canadian treasure. It belonged to the people. You don't want to disturb that which by rights belongs to the people. That would be cruddy."

"So where did you dig?" I ask, getting caught up in the story despite myself.

"In people's backyards. By moonlight. I couldn't even risk a flashlight. During the day I would check out likely-looking backyards. That is to say, ones without dogs. Here, Hershel, see if you can make like a dog." He puts a big steak on Hershel's plate and my mother doesn't even protest that Hershel can't eat that much. This is a *party*.

"Well, I dug and I dug, being careful, of course, to always replace the earth before I left."

"Didn't that kind of make a mess of people's yards?" I ask.

"Aerating," says Ned, and starts cutting enthusiastically into his meat. No one has even bothered with all the side dishes. The steaks are so big that they cover our plates, leaving room for nothing else. The boys have grease all over their faces. They have picked up their steaks and are gnawing on them like little animals but no one cares. We know Ned must have found something and we want to know what.

"Then one day, I hit the jackpot. But it wasn't in someone's backyard. I'd run out of those. It was on the edge of town, well, in a public park, if you want to know. I had to be real careful because that's where the tramps hang out and you don't want to wrestle with a tramp in the dead of night."

"Why not?" asks Max, his eyes huge.

"Tramps are mean, Max," says Ned. "Everyone knows that. I've traveled Canada from one end to the other and a good part of the United States too and I've never met a well-behaved tramp."

"Why not?" asks Maya.

"It's just not in them," says Ned. "Anyhow, so I'm there in the park, digging away in the dead of night, by moonlight, only and keeping one eye out for tramps, when my shovel uncovers it."

There is a long pause as Ned cuts and eats a big piece of steak.

"WHAT?" asks Hershel.

"WHAT?" asks Maya.

"WHAT?" asks Max.

Ned doesn't say anything, just picks up his steak

and dangles it and points at it. It's as if the half-eaten rib steak is a clue. Everyone looks puzzled.

"You dug up a steak?" I ask at last, breaking the solemn silence.

"I don't believe a steak would survive from Viking times," says Ned.

"You dug up a dinosaur?" asks Max.

"You dug up gold like the Mayas," says Maya.

"I dug up a BONE!" says Ned. "Now, what's for dessert?"

"What kind of a bone?" asks Max.

My mother laughs and gets up to clear the table and Ned helps her and as we carry things back to the kitchen we try to get Ned to tell us about the bone but he says it is a cupcake story. And then he says it is a coffee story. And then he says it is a some more wine story. And I finally say that maybe what he needs is time to make up the rest of the story and my mother says, "JANE!" and Ned laughs and says, "Okay, okay." And we move to the porch steps and he says, "Okay, so I dig up this bone. I'm pretty sure it's a thigh bone."

"How did you know?" asks Maya.

"Because it looks like a thigh bone. Hey, I haven't spent my life eating chicken for nothing."

"It looks like a chicken thigh?" asks Max, sounding disappointed.

"Yeah, only like ten hundred times bigger."

"Ten hundred times?"

"Well, slight exaggeration but it was a very big bone. The way you'd expect a *Viking* bone to be. Oh, they were big guys, all right. Big *red*-haired guys."

"Was there red hair on the bone?" asks Hershel.

"No," says Ned. "But, now, this is pretty exciting. I didn't find any namby-pamby bits of pottery or old iron tools or such. I'd found myself a piece of a genuine Viking."

"Oh gross," I say.

"But without the red hair," says Hershel.

"It was still a bone. A *big* bone," says Ned.

"I wish it had some red hair on it," says Max.

"Oh gross," I say again.

"Gross," echoes Maya. I can tell she doesn't really care, she just wants to be on the girls' side.

"Well, it's not like it still had flesh hanging off of it," says Ned. "So anyhow, I think, if I show up with this, here at the local museum, why, they're just going to take it away from me. So I go back to the rooming house where I'm staying and I pack that bone in my knapsack and I get in my car and I head out for the prairies."

"Why the prairies?" I ask.

"Because no one cares what you do on the prairies," says Ned. Then my mother looks down. Hershel is suddenly asleep in the sand. She lifts him gently to put him to bed and Ned watches my mother walking out and the stories seem to leave with her.

"Well, time for more cupcakes," says Ned, and brings the package over. He and Max have two more each and then Max burps and has to lie on his back in the sand. My mother returns and looks at Max and she and Ned laugh.

By the end of the evening, during which time Max and Maya wander off to bed, my mother and Ned have laughed so much they have tired themselves right out and sit on the porch step with their feet half buried in the cool sand. My mother is drawing small pictures with the big toe of her right foot and now and then sighing. She gets up to get her cardigan and then, seeing that I have not gone to bed like the others, invites me down on the steps. She pulls me closer and envelops me in the sweater with her. It is getting a little windy and the sand and salt blow over us but no one suggests moving inside. We just watch the sea turning night colors. Ned won't talk about the bone anymore. He says it's a story for when everyone is awake so we sit in silence for a long time without anyone feeling they have to say anything.

"What a nice place to watch the sun set," says Ned finally.

"Well, I remember you saying that many years before," says my mother dreamily.

It becomes dark out and suddenly I am too tired to sit up so I go to bed. I lie there looking through my lacy dotted swiss curtains, which are gray with age. They have always been in this room. I see my favorite star hanging in the right corner of my window. I pray for Mrs. Nasters over and over but not once for Mrs. Parks.

In the morning I get up and I see Ginny, her feet flying over the sand. I am so glad to see her. I'd hoped we could get together on Saturday.

"Ginny!" I say happily, and then remember that Ned is still sleeping on the couch and run outside to meet her so as not to wake him up.

"Jane!" she says. "Mrs. Parks is in the emergency room!"

Death

My Tenth Adventure

"Oh no, oh no," I say, and then in horror realize how hard I prayed for Mrs. Nasters and how hard I did not pray for Mrs. Parks. To even things up. Now I am afraid to even think anything about anyone. Our prayers are so powerful. Our thoughts are so powerful. "What is wrong with her?"

"No one knows. She woke up in the middle of the night terribly ill and an ambulance came for her! Mrs. Nasters was visiting her. They were having a sleepover. She rode in the ambulance with Mrs. Parks. My mother went into the hospital to see if Mrs. Nasters wanted a lift home. She doesn't really know Mrs. Parks. Mrs. Parks was eating breakfast. She wants your mother to get her car and bring it to the hospital. She also wants some jam."

"She wants jam?" I asked.

"Don't you think you should go and get your mother?"

I run into the house, where my mother is quietly making muffins for breakfast, and I say, "Come *quick*. Mrs. Parks is in the hospital. Mrs. Cavenaugh sent Ginny to tell you, and you are to stop and get Mrs. Parks's car. And bring some jam."

"Everyone likes my jam," says my mother contentedly, but whipping off her apron and grabbing her purse off the hook in the hall. Then she goes over to the couch, where Ned is still snoring away, and shakes his shoulder.

"Something has *happened*," she says to him.

"Whah?" he says in sleeptones.

"Wake up, Ned. I need you to take the muffins out of the oven in fifteen minutes. I have to go to the hospital with Mrs. Parks's car and perhaps bring her home. I wonder if she'd like strawberry or raspberry jam? If you were in the hospital, Ginny, would you rather have strawberry or raspberry jam?"

"Raspberry," says Ginny.

"Strawberry," I say.

"Really?" says my mother. "But what about all those little seeds that get in your teeth? And I suppose she has dentures."

"I'll drive you," says Ned.

"No, you must stay with the muffins," says my mother. "The muffins! The muffins!"

"Also Maya and Hershel and Max," I say.

"Of course," says Ned. He sits up and grabs his car keys off the coffee table by the couch and tosses them to my mother. My mother runs to the pantry and comes out carrying a jar of strawberry and a jar of raspberry jam and holds them up with a questioning look on her face.

"Raspberry," says Ginny.

"Strawberry," I say.

"Both," says Ned.

"Of course, both," says my mother, and we three run down the beach like lightning.

My mother takes Ned's car to Mrs. Parks's house. She needs to get inside to get Mrs. Parks's car keys. The door is locked. Mrs. Nasters must have locked it behind them when the ambulance came. My mother goes to the back door but that is locked too. Finally, after trying all the basement windows, she finds one unlatched. "This is really extremely careless of Mrs. Parks," she says, and leaps into the darkness below.

She screams.

"Are you all right?" I yell down at her.

"Spiders," she calls back, and I can hear her already running up the basement steps. A few seconds later she comes out with the keys and we speed on to Lincoln, where we pull into the parking lot and run to admissions, where we are told it is not yet visiting hours.

"But I was sent for. Anyway, it must be okay for Mrs. Parks to have visitors because Mrs. Nasters was in with her," says my mother.

"Mrs. Nasters is in intensive care," says the receptionist.

"I don't understand. Is Mrs. Parks worse?" says my mother.

"No, Mrs. Parks is fine. The doctors will release her any time now. But Mrs. Nasters had a hemorrhage shortly after she left the hospital and was brought back in by Mrs. Cavenaugh, who was driving her home. Mrs. Cavenaugh has gone on home now," says the receptionist.

My mother shakes her head dumbly and then

asks if she can go up to see Mrs. Nasters. Just as she is saying this, Nellie Phipps comes in. Mrs. Nasters has called for her. We are all somber.

The receptionist phones intensive care and then looks somber herself. "They say you can all go up," she says, and her tone is kinder.

We go up and my mother speaks to the doctor. They can't remove Mrs. Nasters's tumor so they were expecting something like this. She is not doing very well. Suddenly it doesn't seem to matter who I pray for. It is all a mess.

We talk to Mrs. Nasters briefly. She doesn't seem to really notice us much. She asks Nellie to read to her from the Bible but when we leave, Nellie isn't reading. She has her two hands outstretched over her and she is lowering them to Mrs. Nasters's body.

"What in the world is she doing?" asks my mother as we glance back.

"What is she doing?" a nurse whispers to us. Several of them standing around are watching.

I know what Nellie is trying to do but I don't explain and there is no green light coming from her hands to make it evident. Eventually everyone shrugs and goes back to work and we leave to pick up Mrs. Parks, who is being sent home.

"They said there was nothing much wrong with me," says Mrs. Parks when we get to her room. "That's what they said. I'm telling you, it's a conspiracy, and Natalie, Mrs. Nasters, agrees. Just look what happens, they give her a room and they send me home. She doesn't like the situation any better than I do."

My mother sighs. "Mrs. Nasters is really quite ill," she says. "She's in intensive care."

"Oh, they put her in intensive care, did they?" asks Mrs. Parks, her lips pursing. "Well, that just makes me mad enough to spit. Did you bring me jam?"

We drive Mrs. Parks home and settle her in. Then Mrs. Merriweather comes over and my mother tells her about Mrs. Nasters.

"Oh heavens," says Mrs. Merriweather. "Shall I make you some tea, Edna? To have with this nice jam that Felicity brought you?"

This is the first time it occurs to me that Mrs. Parks has a first name. That she had a husband at some time in the distant past. That she may have children somewhere, although I doubt it. Wouldn't they be here now? That she might have done something for a living. And been on committees. That there were trips she took and books she read and theater she went to and disappointments and romances and holiday turkeys. And now, apparently, she is going to start having sleepovers with Mrs. Nasters, her new friend. She is telling us about that now.

"We had it all planned," says Mrs. Parks. "Nellie Phipps came to visit me. Awfully touchy-feely sort she's become. Touching me here. Touching me there. I never knew her to go around calling on her parishioners either. What's gotten into her?"

"I have no idea," says my mother.

"Anyhow, she told me about Mrs. Nasters feeling a bit down in the dumps of late and I invited Natalie to come over and watch some television and keep an eye on me in case the thrombosis, well, *you know*. Then we got tired and I said, Well, I've three spare bedrooms. Why go home? Why not have a sleepover? And Natalie said that she'd be happy to stay and it was a good idea anyhow as we could keep an eye on each other—although it was clear to me there was nothing really very much wrong with *her*. We had Scrabble and we thought we might even order a pizza. It suddenly seemed like . . . fun," said Mrs. Parks as if it had surprised her that she could have that anymore.

"Well," says Mrs. Merriweather, "I'm sure as soon as Mrs. Nasters comes out of the hospital you can have your little sleepover. We'll get you some NIBS or cheese popcorn."

"Don't patronize me, Marjorie," says Mrs. Parks. "And make some tea. I've had a very nasty night."

We leave on that note. Ginny and I talk about what we are going to do but when we get to the house who should we see but Ned and H.K. sitting on the porch together. Ginny says she has to go home for lunch and I don't know if this is true or if she is avoiding the strange men. She turns around and runs back over the sand.

"Oh! H.K.," says my mother. She looks vaguely uncomfortable.

Neither of the men says anything.

"Well!" she says. "Lunch!"

My mother has not had time to pick any orach,

so she sends me and I wade through the reedy shallows by the lagoon. The water is warm on my calves. A heron stands on one leg hunting. There are the hushed sounds of wings on currents of air and the gentle lapping of the water. As if the same energy has taken two forms. The sun does not so much beat down on me as heat the moist air into which I step. I hear sleepy sounds of life everywhere, frogs plopping back into shallows, the buzz of cicadas and flies and dragonflies. I imagine the busy nonstop buzzing day they have, and perhaps they continue all night this way. I have been on the earth twelve years but I don't know how long they sleep. It is funny to think they live next to me, busy busy, and I am so taken up with my own life most of the time, I am not conscious of theirs going on parallel to mine. And they are not conscious of me either or all the important things I think I must do every day.

I sit on a large, smooth rock, letting my calves and feet dry in the sun. I do not know how long I have been there when Maya comes running for me. "WHAT ARE YOU DOING?" she yells. "Lunch is ready."

I grab the little orach I have picked and run back to my mother who throws it into the salad and we all sit down to eat.

"I was sorry you were not able to go antiquing," says H.K. to my mother. "I found quite an interesting pants press."

"Did you, Henry?" says my mother. "I'm sorry as well but Jane was busy and I had no one to leave the children with."

Ned has not looked up from his plate. Now he does. "If you want to go antiquing today, Felicity, I can stay with the kids." He looks at her searchingly.

"That's very good of you, Nate," says H.K.

Ned nods.

"Why don't we all go, Ned? The children too!" says my mother. "And Caroline!"

Ginny has just arrived back on the porch. She obviously did not think lunch would take so long. She is looking through the doorway at all of us, bug-eyed. I don't think she has such interesting turns of events in her house.

"Well, you know, Caroline has not been well lately," says H.K.

"Caroline is Henry's sister," my mother explains to Ned. "She keeps house for H.K."

"I've never had a housekeeper," says Ned. "Of course, I've never had a house."

"My time is not my own since my latest book came out, Nate," says H.K., ducking his head modestly.

"Henry's books do very well," says my mother. "He's really very famous in Massachusetts."

"And other places," says Henry, clearing his throat.

"Yes, I didn't mean to imply that you were a locally known poet only. Like Cassandra Lark," says my mother. "Just that you are *especially* known in Massachusetts. Henry teaches at Simmons."

"Gee, that's swell, Harry," says Ned. "Well, sure, we can all go. Of course, I was going to stay home and tell the children more about the bone."

"Tell us about the bone! Tell us about the bone!" say Hershel and Max and Maya, jumping around Ned.

"No, children," says Ned. "We *must* go antiquing."

"No, tell us about the bone!"

"No, no, Harry isn't interested in Vikings and dinosaurs. Harry likes to decorate."

"Well, of course, if you'd rather stay home and dig up bones with the children . . . ," says H.K.

"Children, go wash your hands. We're all going. I'll just get my purse," says my mother, and we are off.

We split into two cars and drive up the highway to small towns. H.K. does not think it a good idea for us children to go into the antique stores even though Ginny and I are hardly what you would call children. So my mother and Ned and H.K. take turns with us outside the stores entertaining us in other ways.

Ned tells us more about the bone. About how he stayed in a rooming house and left it on the dresser and the maid threw it in the trash and he had to follow its path all the way to the dump and then go digging through the garbage for it with giant rats crawling all around him looking for bones of their own. Hershel and Max like that part especially.

When it is my mother's turn with us, she plays word games. When it is H.K.'s turn he sits silently and makes us sit silently too and says helpful things like "Children, try not to block the entrance. Children, try not to speak too loudly."

Ned takes us into a candy store and when he finds horehound candy is amazed. Then he gets an idea for an article. He says that sometimes he sells small pieces to Canadian magazines and radio. He has the idea to bring Mrs. Parks some horehound candy and see if it sparks memories and write a piece about it. We all try the candy. "This is disgusting," says Ned. We agree. But he thinks maybe people a long time ago liked different things.

My mother's turn again. She takes us to a park.

When it is H.K.'s last turn he sits with us and tells us to close our eyes and he will tell us when it's all over. When we don't do this he closes his eyes and says we can tell him. My mother comes out and asks H.K. why his eyes are closed. He says he has a headache. She asks us children if we are having a good time. Ginny tells my mother this is the best day she has ever had in her entire life and my mother looks at her first with skepticism and then with alarm.

On the way home all of us children want to ride in Ned's car but my mother lets Ginny and me and she rides with the others in H.K.'s. We stop off at Mrs. Parks's. I introduce Ned and he gives Mrs. Parks the bag of horehound candy.

"What's this?" she asks, opening it.

"Well, believe it or not, it's horehound candy!" says Ned.

"Horehound candy? That's very kind of you," says Mrs. Parks. She doesn't sound excited or surprised. I don't think she knows she's supposed to be. She doesn't even sound confused the way you have a right to be if someone you don't know very well suddenly appears on your doorstep with a bag of horehound candy. Maybe when you're that old you've seen it all.

"When is the last time you saw horehound candy?" Ned asks, still fishing for an anecdote.

"Well, never," says Mrs. Parks. "I don't believe I've ever had the pleasure."

"You never had horehound candy in your youth?"

"Never," says Mrs. Parks.

"Are you sure?" asks Ned.

Mrs. Parks is beginning to ruffle but fortunately at that second the phone rings. There is a phone in the foyer and she picks it up. "What? Well, of course you're not sick. That's what I've been saying all along. That you're no sicker than I am. I don't trust any of those doctors as far as I can throw

them. Releasing a poor old woman with a raging
thrombosis and keeping a clearly recovered case
of cancer. It's all too typical, isn't it? Well, of course,
of course I will come and bring you something to
read and your eyeglasses. By my television? All
right, dear. Anything else? Yes, I know. Nellie visited me too. Yes, she gave me this balderdash about
faith healing. Humph. Healing hands. I never
heard such rubbish. My thrombosis is just as raging as always. Yes, I know they say you are better,
but let's face it, Natalie, you weren't very sick to
begin with."

She hangs up. "Honestly, now Mrs. Nasters believes she didn't die because Nellie Phipps came
and healed her. Nellie told me she could feel my
thrombosis shrivel up to nothing and disappear but
I don't buy that kind of bunk. That Phipps family
was always into these strange fringe practices. I believe there was a Phipps who was a snake handler."

Is Mrs. Nasters's recovery proof that Nellie can
heal people just like the channeler and psychic
said? And then it occurs to me. If Nellie can heal,
does that mean she can reverse the damage to
Willie Mae?

Ned says he will drop me at home and get his tape recorder and make a few phone calls in town about this story and then come back and pick up Mrs. Parks. He wants to interview people. If the horehound story isn't going to work out, why, this is even better! Faith healing in Massachusetts!

I think we'd better hurry and find Nellie a place to have her gatherings. After this article comes out, people will probably arrive by the hundreds.

Mrs. Parks puts her horehound candy in her patent leather purse and promises to wait for Ned. They will go to the hospital together and she will introduce him to Mrs. Nasters.

Ned drives me and Ginny to the parking lot and we run back to my house to explain things to my mother while he makes his phone calls. My mother is pleased everyone is better. She is making dinner preparations. H.K. isn't here but whether he has gone home of his own accord or whether my mother has sent him home, we can't tell, and it isn't the type of thing my mother will volunteer. Ginny is staying for dinner so she and I help my mother set the table and play with Hershel and

Max and Maya. It feels happy and like old times. No one is dying.

The sun is leaning heavily in the sky, ready to fall in its nightly plunge, when Ned comes grim-faced across the sand and I see my mother read his expression and go to meet him. He leans into her ear and she stops, her eyes large. Her hands go to her mouth.

They walk toward us. Has Mrs. Naster died after all? But no, it is Mrs. Parks.

The Funeral
My Eleventh Adventure

It is a terrible thing and Ned saw it happen. He was making calls at the public phone booth by the Dairy Queen when a car drove right into its plate glass wall. He rushed over and there was Mrs. Parks slumped over the wheel. He gave her mouth-to-mouth without success until the first responders arrived. At first he thought she must have had a heart attack because although the Dairy Queen's glass wall was ruined, Mrs. Parks didn't have a scratch on her. But no, the paramedics explained to him as they pulled something out of her throat, she had choked on a hard candy. That was probably what caused her to lose control of the car, they speculated.

"She should have waited for me. I could have given her the Heimlich maneuver," says Ned.

"It was probably the thrombosis that finally got her," says my mother.

"It was the horehound," I say, because I'm pretty sure Nellie cured the thrombosis. "The paramedics said she choked on it."

"I suppose the thrombosis might have exploded, causing her to choke on the horehound," says Ned musingly.

"The horehound *we* gave her." I say "we" to be charitable because it was undeniably all his idea.

I wait for the horror of this to hit him so I can console him but it doesn't seem to occur to Ned that maybe he is responsible.

We don't feel much like having a barbecue now. We sit around and eat a little rice.

Later, Mrs. Merriweather comes over and asks my mother if she could do the eulogy. The funeral is to be on Wednesday. Mrs. Parks's only living relative is her sister and she is flying out from California. Mrs. Merriweather called her. My mother says certainly she will do the eulogy.

"Because you're a famous poet," says Mrs. Merriweather.

My mother winces but Mrs. Merriweather doesn't notice.

"I think Mrs. Parks would like having a famous poet do her eulogy and attend her funeral."

"Of course we will be there. We will all be there," says my mother, and then offers Mrs. Merriweather a little rice, but she says she cannot stay. She has other arrangements to make.

"The funeral is scheduled for one o'clock. I've already checked with Nellie," says Mrs. Merriweather.

"One o'clock it is," says my mother.

It will be my first funeral. Then I remember the Gourd children.

"I can't go," I say suddenly. Ned and my mother look down at me.

"Don't be silly," says my mother. "Of course you will be there. We will all be there."

So now I have something new to worry about. I have no idea what to do with the Gourd children. I can hardly bring them to a funeral.

Mr. Fordyce! If he is not going to the funeral maybe he will take them.

It is sober in church the next day. Everyone knows about the terrible accident. I keep waiting for Ned to realize that if he hadn't given Mrs. Parks the candy she wouldn't have died, but he seems to be skating through the service with a clear conscience and a relaxed face.

After church I keep thinking about this, Ned's easy conscience, while we are waiting to shake Nellie's hand—and it is taking a long time because Nellie is not only shaking hands now, she is laying one on each person's shoulder as he leaves. I think she sees herself as a combination of church and free clinic. Finally I can stand it no longer.

"You gave her that candy," I whisper to Ned.

"What?" he says, bending down to hear me better.

"The candy she choked on. If you hadn't given it to her, she wouldn't have died."

"Look, Bibles," he says. He has started calling me this since my mother told him how I deliver Bibles with Nellie. For some reason he finds this hilarious. "If you're going to live, then something is going to have to die to feed you. Everything we eat was alive at some point. Just by *eating* you're going to cause trouble. I figure, every day I'm doing something like giving someone candy they're going to choke on—"

He is interrupted by Nellie, who places a large, meaty hand on his shoulder. He grabs it with both of his, gently removes it and gives it a friendly shake.

"Nellie," I whisper to her when she gets to me. "You did it. You cured Mrs. Nasters and Mrs. Parks. We should find you a gathering place today after we deliver Bibles."

"I could feel that thrombosis break up under these hands. I could feel Mrs. Nasters become whole. Praise Jesus. But I got no time for Bibles or anything else. I've got a funeral to prepare for," Nellie whispers back.

I have a sudden inspiration. "What about the church as a gathering place?"

Nellie looks nervous for a second. Her mouth twitches. "It's *holy* business, this healing, but I don't know as it's exactly *churchly* business, if you know what I mean. Now, move on, move on, you're holding up the line," she says, and yanks me out of the way with the hand she has been using for shaking.

Because I don't have to deliver Bibles I go right

to Mr. Fordyce's. He is sitting at his table reading and eating blueberries. The summer has moved on. I tell him about the funeral and he says of course he will watch the children but I must ask Mrs. Gourd if this is okay with her. I lie and say I will. I have no alternative because I am sure she would say no as it is not the deal we have struck. And I'm sure my mother would say yes, I must come to the funeral.

At dinner the sea is not bloodred but a grim gray. There isn't much conversation. No airplane rides over the sand. No stories of bones. My mother says, "It is very odd that Caroline and H.K. weren't at church. They never miss."

Ned doesn't say anything. He shovels food in and watches the gray water turn to black.

Wednesday I drop the Gourd children at Mr. Fordyce's. He says he is all ready for them. He has gone to the bookstore and bought *Now We Are Six* because he thinks they will like this poetry. He has bought the book *Mud Pies and Other Recipes* because he thinks it would be fun to make mud pies with them. I promise to get them the very second the funeral is out and he says, "Take your time."

At the funeral my mother reads a poem she has written for both the old ladies and their fruited hats. People in the church sigh as they listen to it. Several wipe their eyes. It turns out we all think about the fruited hats and what it means to have them gone. Of course, when my mother wrote the poem she thought Mrs. Nasters was going to die, but Mrs. Nasters, although she will one day die like the rest of us, is, for now, better. It makes the poem slightly less poignant. I think that it is death alone that makes things poignant.

Mrs. Merriweather is sitting next to me. It is only when she bends down and whispers in my ear that I notice how gray her hair is. "These things seem to mark the passing of one generation and the movement along the line for the rest of us, as if we are all on a conveyor belt to death."

"Jesus, lady, lighten up, you're giving me the willies," says Ned.

"Besides, she seems better," I say.

"Shhh," says Mrs. Parks's sister, who is sitting right behind us. "I don't know what you mean by better. She's dead."

"I meant Mrs. Nasters," I explain.

"Shhh," says Mrs. Parks's sister again.

My mother goes on. "Sometimes I think the fated car trip was a blessing. Since the thrombosis was going to take her soon, that when it did she was on the happy errand of going to visit a new friend."

Dr. Callahan looks up suddenly. He is sitting in the front row. He says in a matter-of-fact voice, "That's bursitis, Felicity. Not thrombosis."

"No, I mean what would have killed her eventually, sooner rather than later, she gave us to believe, was the thrombosis. She was very worried about it," says my mother, "which is why I was saying—"

"She didn't HAVE a thrombosis," says Dr. Callahan. "She had bursitis. She came to see me for a couple of simple cases of bursitis. One in her heel and one in her shoulder. Very painful but hardly life-threatening."

Then he folds his hands and goes back to looking

out the window. It is a perfect summer day with wonderful cumulus clouds floating by. All our eyes stray there.

"Oh dear," says my mother. "But . . ." And here she leans down and says this very quietly, meaning to talk only to Dr. Callahan. But it is a small church and we can hear from our seats six rows back. "She thought she had a thrombosis."

"Yes, I know," says Dr. Callahan. "And if I explained the difference once to her, I explained it a dozen times."

"But she said you told her she couldn't travel by air. That her leg would explode."

"Nonsense. I would never say such a foolish thing. What I said was that if she took one of those long-haul flights to California she should get up and walk around. That people get blood clots sometimes from sitting for such lengthy periods. It's what I tell all my patients who take long airplane trips."

"Oh," says my mother.

There is a pause.

"Then there was nothing much wrong with her, really?"

Mrs. Parks's sister speaks up suddenly. "She

wrote to *me* that she had a thrombosis and could not travel. She said *you* told her that."

"Oh, for heaven's sake," says Dr. Callahan.

"Dr. Callahan, please," says my mother, looking worriedly at Mrs. Parks's sister. "I know for a fact that if she could have visited her sister she would have. Why, I was driving her there myself at her request because she believed she couldn't fly."

"Nobody drove to see me," says Mrs. Parks's sister. "I don't know what you're talking about."

"We never got there," mumbles my mother.

"What happened?" demands Mrs. Parks's sister.

"Oh, uh," says my mother, looking uncomfortable, "this and that."

"I'm telling you, she was in the PINK of health," says Dr. Callahan. "And that's what I told her. The pink. The silly fool wanted to go into the hospital. I made the big mistake of telling her that I had just sent Mrs. Nasters there. It is my opinion that you send one old lady to the hospital and they all want to go."

One of the older women in the congregation stands up and leaves the church.

"Really, Dr. Callahan," says my mother mildly.

"All right, all right, the point I'm making is that I wasn't about to send perfectly healthy old ladies to take up beds at our overcrowded hospital. But she just kept demanding to go to Lincoln Memorial."

"I think I can say for certain that my sister had no desire to visit the Lincoln Memorial," says Mrs. Parks's sister, looking more and more confused and upset. "She would have told me *that*."

"I felt her thrombosis break up beneath my hands," bellows Nellie.

"Balderdash," says Dr. Callahan. "She had no thrombosis."

"Everyone seems to think she had one except you," says Mrs. Parks's sister. "It couldn't be that *you're* wrong, could it?"

"Oh *no*, the doctor is *never* wrong," says a little old lady clearly miffed at Dr. Callahan's earlier slight.

"I think it's all been an unfortunate mistake," says my mother quietly.

"Or a case of *very bad communication*," says Mrs. Parks's sister, looking directly at Dr. Callahan.

"I resent that. I did my very best to communicate to Mrs. Parks exactly what was the matter with her but she wasn't having it. I told her clearly she had bursitis. I only told her about the blood clots on plane trips because she said she might be flying to see her sister *if she couldn't get out of it. . . ."*

He pauses here meanly and my mother keeps opening her mouth as if maybe the right words will come out on their own, but they don't.

"MAYBE," says Dr. Callahan, "I should start posting everyone's diagnosis at the town hall so we can all read the straight facts and put a stop to these rumors and people will stop accusing me of telling people they have things that they don't."

"NO!" cry several people in the congregation, and we all turn quickly to see which ones.

"Well, then," says Dr. Callahan with a thin smile.

"Fie on Western medicine!" booms a voice from the back. It is Nellie, who has stood up, but for a second it sounds like the voice of God.

"I'd say that's one doctor who's too big for his britches," says the little old lady.

I find her in the audience and wonder why she isn't wearing a fruited hat.

"Or one preacher who's got delusions of grandeur," says someone else.

"WELL, SHE WAS A DEAR WOMAN AND I

LOVED HER!" shouts my mother above the noise, and this quiets everyone and reminds them why we are here.

There is a somber silence. Someone has died. Everyone sits quietly for a few minutes. It does not matter suddenly who believes what or who is wrong and in the stillness of that church we say goodbye.

Later, as everyone is filing out, Mrs. Parks's sister is heard saying that she expected better from a famous poet.

Ned puts his arm around my mother's shoulders and heads down the aisle of the church. My mother promises Mrs. Parks's sister that she will help her clean out Mrs. Parks's house on Saturday and this mollifies her somewhat. "Well," says the sister, sniffing disdainfully. "I suppose really that eulogies are hard to do. I suppose you did the best you could."

"Well, of course I did," says my mother, and Ned leads her out.

When they get outside Ned asks my mother

what she wants to do but she looks preoccupied and doesn't seem to hear him. She is watching people leave the church and craning her neck as if looking for someone.

"Not here again," she says worriedly. "Neither of them. Not Henry and not Caroline. I wonder why."

Ned looks suddenly worried as well.

Everyone Disappears
My Twelfth Adventure

The Blackberries Are Ripe

Saturday morning Ned is gone. I notice it first. I am eating blackberries that my mother has been picking around the house, hoping to get to them before the birds do. She comes in with some more and I say, "Are you going to make blackberry jam soon?"

The pantry shelves are lined with blueberry jam jars under the raspberry under the strawberry. My mother says, "Shhh, you'll wake Ned."

"He's not here," I say. "He was gone when I got up."

My mother pulls the living room curtains then and the room is awash in morning light. All traces of Ned are gone.

"Did he tell you he was going?" I ask anxiously.

"No. Be careful and wipe up the smears on the table," says my mother because I have mistakenly put my elbow on a blackberry and it leaves a large purple streak. "Blackberries stain so. Are you going to help me clean out Mrs. Parks's house?"

"Can Ginny come too?" I ask.

"Of course," says my mother. "Hurry and get her and I'll meet you there."

"What about Maya and Hershel and Max?" I ask. "If Ned is gone."

"Oh yes," says my mother vaguely. She is bustling around with laundry baskets and berries and mops, getting the day in order. "Well, I guess we'll just have to take them along. What is Mrs. Parks's sister going to do with those geese?"

"Where did Ned go?" I ask, thinking I shouldn't ask.

"Oh, I don't know," says my mother. "Here." She hands me a cloth to clean up the smushed berry.

"Don't you want to know?" His suitcase, which always sits littering the coffee table, is gone now too.

"Well, he has a tendency to just disappear. At least he used to."

"You mean he's gone for good? Just like that?"

"Could be," says my mother, but she seems more concerned about getting Maya and Hershel and Max, who have just awoken, fed and dressed. They will have to walk to Mrs. Parks's now, I realize. Ned's car had been nice.

I run to the new development to find Ginny and bring her to Mrs. Parks's and by the time we get there my mother is already knee-deep in piles of things that they are sorting for Goodwill and the garbage. Mrs. Parks's sister is taking little back with her to California.

We come upon a whole closet of wonderful dresses and shoes from some period of Mrs. Parks's dress-up life. They are beaded and chiffony.

"Wow," says Ginny, reading a label. "Valentino."

"My sister's first husband was a movie producer," says Mrs. Parks's sister. "She was only married to him for three years." She whispers something in my mother's ear and my mother's eyes get large. Then Mrs. Parks's sister resumes her normal tones. "All she took away from that marriage were these wonderful clothes. Still, I'm surprised she kept them all these years. I wouldn't think she'd want to

206 ---- my one hundred adventures

remember. Gee, what to do with them? They're not really Goodwill and they're certainly not garbage."

"Can I have them?" asks Ginny, and her cheeks are flushed. "Please."

"I guess they *would* make wonderful dress-up clothes," says Mrs. Parks's sister. "Yes, take them. I'm not carting them all the way to California, that's for sure."

"Some of these are probably worth a lot of money," says my mother, holding up something that even I can tell is just wonderful.

"Ech," says Mrs. Parks's sister. "Maybe. If I wanted to go to all that bother. But I plan to dispose of all of this before I fly back. Let the girls have them for play."

"I'm not going to play dress-up," says Ginny. "I would never use these for something like that. These are art. I'm going to study them. These are like a textbook, do you understand?"

"No," says Mrs. Parks's sister, not looking very interested either.

"Ginny wants to be a dress designer," I say.

We are examining everything and tripping on things and generally getting in the way when there is a scream from outside. A goose has bitten Hershel and he's bleeding. My mother calms him down and asks Ginny and me if we will please take him and Max and Maya to the beach.

So we take all the designer clothes and Max and Hershel and Maya and drop the clothes at Ginny's house. She grabs her sketchbook and we head with the children down to the beach, where Ginny says, "I was in such despair, Jane. All I had in my life was soccer camp. Everything I wanted to do this summer was destroyed. Now I can come home every night and know that I have these clothes to study. It makes all the difference, do you understand? I can see firsthand how they are finished, how they are tailored, how they are designed. I had almost given up but now this is a *sign*. You believe in signs, don't you?"

I say I don't know if there are signs but everybody seems to be looking for them.

Max and Hershel keep coming up to me and Ginny and complaining. We are not fun like Ned. He builds them forts. He makes them tunnels. We just sit there and yap together.

So Ginny decides we will build them a boat. She

gets some driftwood and goes to her house for nails and a hammer from her garage. She and I nail together a raft. It is quite respectable-looking. Then she gets a piece of kelp and hands one end to Hershel. The big, bulbous end she buries under a rock on the shore. The sea is calm today with practically no waves.

"My mom doesn't let them in the water without an adult," I say worriedly.

"They aren't in the water, they're on a raft," she says. "Besides, look. I have it anchored with that rock and as long as Hershel doesn't let go of his end they won't go anywhere. And Hershel, you're not going to let go of your end, are you?" she asks with such a scary face that he just shakes his head, his eyes large with worry.

"Good boy. Now you can pretend you are sailing to China."

She and I go back to sketching dresses. She sketches some of Mrs. Parks's dresses and then shows how she could design something similar based on them. Maya has her own little game going with some gull feathers and beads that Ginny has given her. She is talking quietly to herself.

We grow tired and lie on our towels soaking up sun and I think Ginny is sketching but when I look up later she has fallen asleep.

I hear, "Whale! Whale!" now and then but I am so used to Max saying this that I pay no attention. Then through my sun-soaked fog I realize it is not Max but Maya. And Maya never calls "Whales!"

I turn. The boys' raft is no longer floating attached to the shore. Hershel has forgotten to hang on to the kelp, and the raft is out to sea. And they are not alone. There is a whale. I see just the tip of the tail as it goes under. It is too close to the raft but the boys don't notice it because they are facing the wrong way. Beyond them further out is a rowboat and in it, what I am sure is the clothes hanger man, still in his too-big suit. Even in my panic it occurs to me that it is an odd thing to wear rowing. He is making his way to the boys.

I do not even bother to wake Ginny. I make not a sound because there is no time or spit for it but run into the water and start to swim toward the raft. The boys see me coming and smile and point. They don't seem to care that they are drifting out to sea. They are idiots. I am suddenly furious at them but know I cannot say anything to panic them. I am glad they are idiots. They will stay calm. I do not know who will get to them first, the whale, the clothes hanger man or me.

Just as I grab the edge of the raft and start to signal with one hand to the clothes hanger man that I have it, a huge crest of water arises behind the rowboat. The rowboat lifts with the powerful wake as the whale surfaces and I hear the clothes hanger man cry, "Maaaaaaaaaax!" Then the boat, the whale and the man all go under together.

I watch only a second before swimming as hard as I can to shore, towing the raft. Max and Hershel still have not seen what I have seen. Maya is standing on the shore looking stunned.

I get the boys to shore and shout for Ginny, who has just woken and turns reluctantly to view me dripping in the shallows and then leaps to her feet.

I scan the ocean but there is nothing. "We have to get the sheriff," I yell to her, explaining and panting as she runs to me.

I stay with the children and Ginny goes to town. After a bit the sheriff's car appears with Ginny and my mother, who they picked up at Mrs. Parks's. My mother puts her arms around me immediately. I am shaking and crying and I tell them what I saw. Ginny has already told the sheriff, who has called out the coast guard. He says there is nothing else to be done and for us to go home, he will let us know when he hears something.

We all go back to our house and sit on the steps and my mother keeps asking me if I am sure I saw a man in a boat. If I am sure it was the clothes hanger man. I tell her how he cried "Max" right before the boat went under and my mother drops her face into her hands and says nothing.

There are helicopters and boats but later the sheriff comes over and tells us they have found no traces of anything. Not a boat or a man or a whale. Was I *sure* I saw those things? Maya saw the whale but she doesn't remember the boat. "How could you not see the boat?" I ask her over and over. The sheriff repeats, a little more skeptically, that they found nothing. But the sea is so large it can swallow anything: your stories, your dreams, your past, your father.

Ginny is shivering and we walk her home. My

mother tells Ginny's mother what has happened and Ginny's mother rolls her eyes. She definitely doesn't believe us. She sees the pile of old clothes in the front hall and her lips become very tight but she just tells Ginny to quickly run a bath, she's getting sand on the carpet.

We go home and make dinner and go to bed, same as always. We say nothing to Max or Hershel, who are very pleased with themselves and their big adventure. Maya is not bothered by any of it. She takes her feathers and beads to bed.

In the middle of the night I wake up to hear a strange noise. At first it is nose blowing as if someone has a terrible cold, and then I realize it is the sound of my mother crying. It goes on and on and I hear my mother's feet pacing, as if she is scurrying down a trail into the night, and I wonder who my mother is looking for there, H.K. or Ned or the clothes hanger man.

There is a long time now as summer drifts on. No one has said anything else about the clothes hanger man. My mother is afraid, I think, to believe I was right and she will not simply believe I was wrong, but she can believe I may have been mistaken. The sheriff cannot trace him because he was a vagrant. If that was his car we saw, there doesn't seem to be a registration in his name. I don't think the sheriff believes me anyhow, he is just doing his job. I wonder what kind of life the clothes hanger man has had that he can disappear so easily from the earth. There is something about the freedom of this that I like as well. As if he lived his life like a dandelion seed floating in the wind. That for all the fuss and funerals, the truth is we all slip in and out exactly this way.

If he was my father, I alone saw him die. If he was Maya's or Hershel's or Max's, I witnessed this for them, but they will probably never believe me either. I cannot do anything about this and I did not know him well enough to mourn.

I bring Willie Mae to Nellie for faith healing even though I am doubtful about the outcome. Surely, though, if Nellie *can* heal, this will solve everything. But knowing exactly what Nellie does, it seems a little wrong to give her a *baby* to practice on. Suppose she cannot, after all, do what she says? Suppose Dr. Callahan was right and there never was a thrombosis?

I ask Nellie if she is sure she can heal people and she says I have to have faith and I think I do, but not necessarily in Nellie. Nellie sees me hestitating and grabs the baby carrier. Willie Mae's purple bruise and bump have long since disappeared but Nellie moves her hands around over him. After a bit she says she can feel the part of the brain that was damaged and she has healed it.

Maybe she has and maybe she hasn't. We have no proof. I want to tell Mrs. Gourd that there will be no long-term effects of the injury, that Nellie averted any problems in this area. Maybe I just want so desperately to find proof of *something* that I will believe anything at all.

Nellie has been twice to the lake to find the transporting poodle without luck. Also, not as many people have come to her for miraculous healing as she thought would. I tell her not to worry, that word will spread and they will come. I am trying to be supportive. She talks all the time now about who is evolved and who is not and where she thinks they are in terms of some kind of hierarchy of goodness. It makes me nervous. It seems to me that she doesn't think it takes much to slip up.

Church seems sad and empty and hatless. Mrs. Nasters is on a slow decline again and back in the hospital. I ask Nellie about this and she says healing doesn't come with a warranty. Sometimes it only lasts so long.

Ginny says she has hidden the dresses from her mother. Her mother thinks they are filthy things and wanted Ginny to throw them away so Ginny told her she had and hid them under her bed. Her mother never vacuums there, she says; they are safe.

We do not hear from Ned. H.K. comes over now and then. I think my mother may be thinking romantically of him after all. They take walks. She is not happy around him as she was around Ned. There is no party atmosphere. But Ned is gone.

Most importantly, my mother never finds out what I have done. Mrs. Gourd has kept her word as we have kept ours and no one knows how I have almost ruined a life. So for now the house is still ours. But there is no joy. The house is no longer a sanctuary. It may not always be a member of our family. It may be taken from us as no family member could be, so what is it, then? Just a house. I cannot afford to love it anymore.

Summer is sliding to an end. There are only a few weeks left. The blackberries are really ripening now, the bushes heavy with them. It is hard to tell with blackberries which are truly ripe. They can appear dark and plump but when you pop one in your mouth, you feel the little buds' resistance and a sourness shocks your tongue. Another equally dark berry can instead burst into a sweet, mysterious, complicated flavor. It is better to wait until you are sure they are all ripe or past ripeness but we cannot wait. We pick them. My mother makes a pie and some jam but there is not enough for a lot of jam yet. It is the last shelf of summer to fill. The strawberry, raspberry and blueberry shelves are replete. Their time is done.

I begin to worry how I will babysit when school starts and what will happen if I cannot. Will Mrs. Gourd go to my mother after all? Will all this loss of summer's freedom be for nothing? I wake up in the middle of the night now and watch the moon and twist in my bed with worry. Maya breathes deeply, warmly, in the bed on the opposite wall. In her innocence she glides into dreams. She has not asked for adventures. She has not had the chance to ruin her life. Or ours. I do not know if I envy her her state. It would be good to be without this knowledge of what I have done. But to give up the adventures for it? To not have driven into the night with Mrs. Parks and a heart buzzing with excitement?

On Saturday I meet Ginny on the steps of Russel's drugstore. Her grandmother has sent her a hundred dollars as she does from time to time. Ginny is supposed to put it in the bank for her college education but sometimes she spends part of it. We buy a bottle of bubbles, two bottles of pop and some string licorice. We sit on the steps and blow bubbles until a man tells us to move along, we are blocking his passage, and then we go to the grocery store's steps. They are much wider. People can easily go around us. We watch people walk by and notice a dog that is tied to a mailbox. I would like to have a dog, I say to Ginny. She says she likes dogs but her mother will never allow it. Too messy.

I tell Ginny everything I have thought about in the night. She is silent and blows bubbles.

"If your mother marries H.K. then she doesn't have to worry about losing the house. If Mrs. Gourd sues, H.K. can pay her off," says Ginny finally.

"My mother cannot marry H.K.," I say. "It would be too terrible. He would never live at the beach house."

"Why not? Everyone wants a house on the beach if they can afford it."

"I don't think he likes sand and besides, what about Caroline?"

"He should ditch Caroline. Or better yet, he should put her in a proper mental institution. Everyone knows she's completely crazy. She has been making H.K.'s life a trial for years. I'm sure if your mother were to marry H.K., the first thing they would do is put Caroline in a mental institution."

"My mother would never tell H.K. to do that."

"Well, *you* should. You should sit him down and tell him that if he wants a chance with your mother he will have to get rid of Caroline first."

"I couldn't," I say. I don't want to even entertain the idea that things have gone that far, let alone encourage them.

"Well, I could and I think I just might," says Ginny in her reckless way, and then a lemon falls on her head.

We look up and gasp. Towering silently behind us, two paper bags loaded with groceries in her arms, is crazy Caroline. We do not know how long she has been standing there. Long enough, apparently. Her breath is coming in short, sharp bursts, like a bull's. Her eyes are huge and full of hatred. She seems hardly aware of the groceries, she is so upset, and things spill from the bags and down the steps.

Ginny doesn't even think, she gets up, drops and spills the bubbles all over the pavement and races for the beach. I follow. We have left the drinks and licorice behind. We run until our legs give out and we fall in the sand. When we turn we are relieved to see that Caroline has not pursued us.

"Oh my God," says Ginny, panting. "Did you see her face? Oh my God."

We are so flustered we do not even go back for the drinks and licorice or to clean up the bubbles. We walk rapidly to my house and close both doors because Caroline knows where I live. Then we sit and watch my mother making jam. Stirring berries. Singing to herself. She wants to know why we closed the outside door. It hasn't been closed all summer. We say we don't know.

After that we go with her to the marsh, where we spot birds and breathe in the mucky smell and feel our feet sink deeply into the welcoming, warm mud.

At dinnertime Ginny goes home.

The next morning we are getting out of church when Mrs. Cavenaugh comes racing up to us on the church steps.

"Where is she?" she says to me. She is panting even though she has driven over.

"Who?" I ask.

"Ginny. Where is she? Did she go to church with you?"

"No," I say.

My mother frowns and pulls Mrs. Cavenaugh and me away from everyone else. Maya is hanging on her hand. "What has happened?" my mother asks Mrs. Cavenaugh. "Can't you find Ginny?"

"No, I can't," says Mrs. Cavenaugh. "She never came out of her room this morning. I thought she was tired. I thought she was sleeping so I didn't even look in on her. Then when she wasn't up by eleven I got worried so I poked my head in the door and her bed was made and she wasn't there. I hadn't even heard her come downstairs and I was up by eight. What would she be doing leaving the house so early in the morning if she wasn't going to see you? I was *SURE* she was with you."

"We haven't seen her at all," says my mother.

"I suppose you think I'm making a big fuss over nothing," says Mrs. Cavenaugh in fury.

"Oh no," says my mother. "If I woke up and Jane was missing, I would be beside myself with worry. I would be frantic."

"I must tell Mr. Cavenaugh you don't know where Ginny is. We must, we must call the police!" says Mrs. Cavenaugh. "Where else could she be? She's a completely reliable, sensible child. She wouldn't just run off. She may have been kidnapped! We must call the sheriff immediately!"

My mother's eyes grow big at this. Kidnapping has never occurred to either of us. My mother turns to me solemnly.

"Did Ginny say *anything* to you yesterday? Anything about going anyplace? Was she upset about anything?" she asks me. "Were there any strange skulking characters hanging out around the two of you when you were out together? THINK, JANE!"

When she says "strange skulking characters" the first thought that pops into my mind is the cigarette man. That's how crazy and upset I am, because that turned out to be Ned, of course. We can eliminate him. And he's the only strange person I have seen in town. What am I saying? I was thinking of strange people we don't know but there is someone else. Someone strange we do know. I look toward the church and goose bumps rise on my skin.

"Where was H.K. today?" I say. "Where was Caroline?"

"What does she mean?" Mrs. Cavenaugh asks my mother, gripping her forearm so hard she leaves nail marks.

"The poet H. K. Thomson has been missing church lately but he wouldn't kidnap anyone," says my mother.

"Not H.K.," I shout, but no one says to calm

down, *"Caroline!"* And I relate what happened on the steps of the grocery store, leaving out the part about H.K. and my mother getting married and only telling about how Ginny wanted to go to H.K. and suggest he put Caroline away. "And Caroline wasn't in church either!"

"Let's not leap to conclusions," says my mother. "But we must certainly get the sheriff and go to Caroline's house to be sure."

Mrs. Cavenaugh is already on her feet and running to her car.

"Don't go to the house alone. Wait for the sheriff!" my mother calls, but it is useless, Mrs. Cavenaugh is already pointed in that direction. My mother lets go of Maya's hand and starts running for the sheriff's office, calling over her shoulder, "Stay with Maya and Max and Hershel, Jane!"

I go to the side of the church, where Hershel and Max are drawing with twigs in the sand, and I bring them over to Nellie, who is still blessing people.

"I can't deliver Bibles, Nellie," I begin, but she interrupts.

"I'm busy here. Go wait by the Sunday-school room. I have a special route for us picked out."

"I can't. This is an emergency. Ginny is missing. She may have been kidnapped!"

Everyone is staring at me now. Maya begins to cry. Hershel puts a thumb in his mouth. "Please just watch Maya and Hershel and Max for me. Please take them home with you. You can park them in front of the television. They won't be any trouble. I'll come for them later."

"Nonsense, child. There's nothing you can do about that girl. Come with me and let the grown-ups handle it."

"Please watch Maya and Hershel and Max," I say. "I'll be back in an hour!"

I am so sure that Nellie is just thinking too slowly for the moment and will understand any second, that I simply leave Maya and Max and Hershel with her and run after my mother to the sheriff's office.

When I get there my mother is climbing into his car.

"Quick!" she calls to me, and I hop in the back. "Who is watching the children?"

"Nellie," I say, panting, and she nods.

As we drive over to Caroline and H.K.'s house,

the sheriff makes me tell him the whole story about
what happened on the steps of the grocery store.
But again I leave out the part where Ginny and I
talked about my mother and H.K. getting married
and moving to the beach house without Caroline
so that he says finally, "It seems kind of thin to me.
Why would Caroline think H.K. would listen to a
couple of girls?"

"I don't know. It's just what happened," I say, and
mention her crazy, angry eyes.

"Aren't you the same girls who claim you saw a
man in a boat disappear just a couple of weeks
ago?"

"That was me, not Ginny," I say in a low voice.

"And no body was ever found. And no boat rem-
nants and no whale seen either. You girls aren't
trying to scare up a little summer excitement for
yourselves, are you? I'm not going to find Ginny
hiding somewhere while we get the whole town
stirred up, am I? Or off with some boy?"

My mother, who is riding in the front seat next
to the sheriff, turns around and gives me a sympa-
thetic look.

I burst into tears.

"Well, it's probably nothing," says the sheriff in a nicer tone. "Girls apt to go off and do silly things at your age, no offense, Jane. And as for H.K. and Caroline not coming to church, you-all don't have a phone down there on the beach so there's no way for them to let you know if they changed their plans. Simplest explanation is usually the right one. Ockham's razor."

I am not consoled by this because to me the simplest explanation is that Caroline has killed everyone with an axe.

When we get to Caroline's house, Ginny's mom is pounding on the door and shrieking for Caroline, H.K. and Ginny like a madwoman. But no one is answering. The sheriff looks into the open garage. H.K.'s car is gone.

"Looks like they went somewhere," he says.

Then we hear a crash inside the house.

"Someone's in there!" shouts Mrs. Cavenaugh. "GINNY! GINNY! I'm going in!" She puts a rock through the living room window.

"Whoa! Whoa! For God's sake, try the door first, Katrina!" says the sheriff, grabbing Mrs. Cavenaugh's arm and pulling her back away from the house. "I guess we've got exigent circumstances. Now you let me. Let's go see if the back door is open."

We run around the back and sure enough the door opens when he turns the handle.

He calls, "Caroline!" and when no one answers, he frowns and tells us to stay outside, but Mrs. Cavenaugh ignores him. We wait, and then hear Mrs. Cavenaugh scream. My mother tells me to stay where I am and runs into the house.

A few minutes later the sheriff comes out with a sobbing, wild-eyed, hairless Caroline. He puts her in the car and speeds away.

My mother comes out with her arm around Mrs. Cavenaugh, who is stiff as a board. "Jane, we're going back to Ginny's house. Ginny isn't here. The sheriff is going to take Caroline to a hospital."

"Where's Ginny?" I ask stupidly.

"Shhh," says my mother. "I'll tell you about it when we get Ginny's mother home. The sheriff is going to meet us there in a bit."

When we get to Ginny's house her mom falls crying into the arms of her dad, who has been waiting by the phone in case Ginny or someone else calls. But no one has.

My mother takes me onto the front steps and explains that H.K. has eloped with one of his graduate students and left Caroline a note. Caroline has been living alone for days since it happened and they found her medication thrown all over the floor along with the hair she shaved off her head and two bags of spilled groceries, most of which were lemons. She had bought six dozen lemons.

"Caroline doesn't know anything about Ginny. She doesn't even seem to know who she is. She wouldn't really be too aware of much since she stopped taking her pills."

"But then where is Ginny?" I say.

"We don't know," says my mother.

We go back inside. She makes Mr. and Mrs. Cavenaugh tea and they thank her but they don't pick up the cups.

Eventually the sheriff comes and we all sit in the living room while Ginny's mom shreds Kleenex and I try to think where in the world Ginny could have gone or how someone could have gotten ahold of her. Mr. Cavenaugh gets up and paces. Then he sits back down close to the phone. The sheriff has called in help but for now his job is to wait with the Cavenaughs. Mrs. Cavenaugh's eyes look like glass. My hands have cold sweat on them. My mother keeps getting up and making more tea and throwing out the old. Then the phone rings. Everyone in the room jumps.

Mr. and Mrs. Cavenaugh both leap on the phone, grabbing it so violently that I think they are going to fight over it, but Mr. Cavenaugh lets Mrs. Cavenaugh answer.

"Oh thank God. Oh thank God," says Mrs. Cavenaugh over and over. "When did you get her? Is she okay? Yes. Yes. We'll be there soon."

My mother pulls my sleeve and we tiptoe outside to sit on the steps. Wherever Ginny is, she is obviously okay.

"This has been a terrible day," says my mother, finally dropping her head into her hands.

I wonder how much of it has to do with H.K. eloping or if she has even had time to digest this yet.

At last the sheriff comes out on the porch and tells us that Ginny used the money from her grandmother to buy a bus ticket to New York early this morning. When she got to the Port Authority terminal, she called her aunt Lucy, who lives there, to come get her. And as soon as her aunt had her safely in tow and found out she hadn't told her parents, she called them.

The sheriff shakes his head. "I don't know what she was thinking but I suppose I never will. That's one of the things I never get used to on this job, not finding out the ends of stories if they end well. Oh well, at least this one *did* end well. Just as I said, girls your age apt to do silly things. Can I give you folks a lift somewhere?"

Mr. and Mrs. Cavenaugh are off to New York City to pick up Ginny and bring her home.

"Could you give us a ride to Nellie Phipps's house?" asks my mother. "Is that where Nellie was taking the children, Jane?"

"I don't know," I say. "I just left them with her. She's probably there or still at the church."

But we go to both places and they aren't at either and Nellie's car is gone.

"Darn it all," I say. "She must have taken them with her to deliver Bibles. I *told* her I'd be back in an hour." I am unbelievably tired suddenly and just

want everyone together and home before someone else disappears.

"Oh well, at least you know where they are and
that they'll be safe with Nellie. She's no Caroline.
What was Caroline thinking? My, my," clucks the
sheriff. "If I were Mr. Thomson I'd be concerned
about that woman."

"I'd be more concerned about Henry. What was
he thinking, leaving Caroline there all alone with
just a note?" says my mother.

"I guess she just snapped," says the sheriff.

"Or he did," says my mother as we drive back to
the parking lot on the beach.

"There was some talk, you know, that *you* were
his latest girlfriend," says the sheriff. I wonder if
they have forgotten that I am in the backseat.

"I imagine he encouraged that so he could elope
with this student without Caroline interfering,"
says my mother. "He certainly never let on to me
that he was going to get married. But then we
didn't really have such intimate conversations. We
mostly just talked of this and that. This and that."

The sheriff stops the car by the beach and we
get out and thank him.

"Come on," says my mother to me after he has pulled away. "We may as well go home and have some lunch and wait for Nellie to return the children."

But hours pass and by suppertime Maya and Max and Hershel still haven't shown up and my mother is getting antsy.

"Maybe she took them home with her and is waiting for us to collect them?" she says. "Did you iron out any plans when you asked her to watch them?"

"No, I just said I'd get them in an hour."

"Could you run to her house, Jane, and see if they're all back? It's getting late."

So I run across the sand and through town and when I get to Nellie's house her car is in the drive and I think, Thank goodness, let this day be over. I knock on the door and when she appears I hear she is watching television and I ask for Maya and Hershel and Max and she says, "Well, I don't have them, child."

"Where are they?" I ask.

"I gave them to Mrs. Martin as soon as you took off. She does babysitting. I don't. I don't know what you thought you were doing leaving them with *me*."

"Mrs. Martin?" I say.

"You know Mrs. Martin. She babysits. Your mother used to hire her when you were little."

I stand openmouthed. I had forgotten Mrs. Martin until I saw her name in Mr. Fordyce's book. Now here she is again. The way you learn a new word and then suddenly see it everywhere.

"Go on, child. They're probably at her house right now."

"Probably? Miss Phipps! And I don't even know where she lives," I say, exasperated. It is becoming twilight. I am exhausted. I don't want to have to go searching for someone's house.

Nellie looks up the address, writes it down, hands it to me and then closes the door.

I have to find Mulberry Street and when I do finally get to the right house and Mrs. Martin opens the door, there are Hershel and Max and Maya all looking very unhappy.

"Oh my goodness, little Jane Fielding. I used to sit with you when you were about Max's age and then with your brothers and sister too as they came along. I just love babies but my, they can be work. Your poor mother really needed to get out of the house in those days."

I just stare at her.

"That will be six hours at seven dollars an hour for forty-two dollars. Do you need a receipt?" asks Mrs. Martin.

I can't say anything but it doesn't seem to bother her.

"Did your mother forget to send money with you?" she asks, looking down at me understand-ingly. She seems like a nice woman but this is *so* much money.

"Yes," I say, answering her money question the easiest way.

"Look at how you've all grown. I bet you don't remember me, do you, dear?"

I want to snap, How could I remember, I was Max's age and asleep. I am becoming dangerously frayed.

"Never mind. I'll settle up with your mother when I see her next," she says, and I am so stunned that I don't even say thank you. I just take Maya and Hershel and Max and leave.

"I want to go home," says Max over and over.

"We *are* going home," I reply over and over. I don't mind repeating the same thing. I can do it automatically without paying them much attention because now that I finally have the children back, the enormity of what Nellie has done, or rather *not* done, hits me and I am seething.

I have been so willing to accept that everything Nellie does must be for good purpose because she is so obsessed with positive and negative energy. I wanted to believe that she knew more than me. That she was the way to find *something*. I want to think it's okay that she wouldn't babysit; that she has evolved reasons. But it isn't okay.

I have delivered Bibles with Nellie. I have walked around lakes looking for transparent poodles and encouraged her faith healing and dreamt up gathering places. I have looked up to her as knowing about moving energy and the working of the universe. I have encouraged her belief in her healing hands when others wouldn't. I have tried to take her word for it against my own good sense and judgment. I thought she was my friend.

But now I realize that Nellie has no interest in

me. She is too busy chasing the divine. How can a person, if she is so evolved, ignore a simple request from someone really in need? How can she heal people with her hands if she can't even watch three children for an hour during a crisis? This isn't a friend, I think. This isn't a holy person. This isn't even someone who is very nice. This is just someone who wants some spiritual excitement and a warm body along to believe in her.

I know I will never deliver Bibles with Nellie again.

Everyone Reappears
My Thirteenth Adventure

It is three days later and Ginny has returned from New York. She does not have to go to soccer camp this week. I think her mother has given up that idea. We are lying on the beach watching the Gourd children and laughing at poor Dr. Callahan. Every summer we watch him try to take his vacation and lie on the beach and read and relax but because people needing medical advice now must go all the way to Lincoln, they come sniffling and coughing with towels, which they put down suspiciously close to his, and before long he is working again.

"I don't know why he just doesn't vacation somewhere else. Aren't doctors rich?" asks Ginny.

238 ---- my one hundred adventures

"Maybe he likes it," I say. "Maybe he is one of those people who can't really take time off."

Ginny frowns and looks out at the ocean. "I think I will be one of those people," she says. "I'm not really happy unless I'm designing clothes or making them."

Ginny has told me what happened. Her mother found the vintage clothes under the bed after all. It turns out that she does vacuum under beds from time to time. When Ginny got home Saturday from our house and reached under the bed to take out the clothes, they were gone. Her mother had hauled them to the dump with a load of other things. And she wouldn't take Ginny there to retrieve them. And neither would her father. Her parents said the clothes would be covered with garbage and rats.

"I remembered what you said about people's fires. I knew my mother didn't care about mine but I never thought she would try to extinguish it. Things will never be the same between us after this," says Ginny.

"But what were you going to do in New York?" I asked.

"I didn't think that part through. I was just so

mad. I decided not to wait any longer. Just to go. I had this vague plan that my aunt Lucy would let me live with her."

"I am done with Nellie Phipps the way you are done with your mother but while I was with her she claimed to have healed Willie Mae."

"Oh, for heaven's sake," scoffs Ginny.

"There's no way of knowing for sure," I say.

"Hey, listen, I don't believe it for a second but if you do, what are we doing still babysitting the Gourds? We have two weeks of vacation left," says Ginny.

"We have no proof we can give Mrs. Gourd that Willie Mae won't grow up damaged from the Bible I dropped. And as long as we have no proof she could still sue."

"How do we know there *is* no way to get proof? Maybe there are tests the doctors can give Willie Mae."

"Don't you think Mrs. Gourd would have thought of that already?"

"Mrs. Gourd? Are you kidding? Feh. She'd probably never even ask about such tests. But we can. Dr. Callahan is right here."

"He won't know," I said.

"He might."

And before I can say anything Ginny has plopped herself right next to him. "Dr. Callahan," she says in a loud voice. His eyes are shut. I think he is pretending to be asleep. "Dr. Callahan! Are there any tests you can give Willie Mae to find out if he's going to be developmentally challenged from the Bible that got dropped on his head?"

Dr. Callahan sits up and frowns at her. "What are you nattering about?" he asks, putting a hand over his eyes to shield them from the sun and squinting at her.

"Don't you remember at the beginning of the summer when Jane dropped a Bible on Willie Mae's head? Mrs. Gourd came out of the checkup with Willie Mae and you told Jane that Mrs. Gourd could sue her for it? He had a bump and a bruise on his forehead?"

"I remember that checkup. Yes. Well, there's no damage, for heaven's sake. And he didn't get the bump from some Bible. He got it when I asked Mrs. Gourd to hand me my stethoscope and she dropped it on Willie Mae's head. Thirty years of practice and I've never had a mother drop something on her own baby's head. Remarkable."

I sit there like stone.

"He didn't come in with the bump?" asks Ginny, turning her head to look at me.

"No, he came in just fine. He *left* with a big black-and-blue mark and a bump, but again, parents are lucky that babies are made of rubber. Most of the things that happen to them bounce right off. And certainly no one is going to be developmentally challenged from a little bruise like that. Particularly on that part of the skull. Skulls are interesting. Head injuries are interesting. Hit the skull in this place and it cracks like an eggshell and the person bleeds into the brain and it's all over. Hit them an inch to the right and there's no damage to the skull at all. As I say, interesting. But even if she'd dropped the stethoscope on a fragile part of the skull, she didn't drop it hard enough to do anything but make a nice dramatic goose egg, which, although stunningly purple, was nothing more than a little boo-boo, really. Now can you please move? You're in my sun."

All those nights of twisting in bed, worried. My whole ruined life. It is like waking from a bad dream. At first I am elated.

Then Ginny, who does not look elated, only

mad, thanks Dr. Callahan, returns to me and says, "We've been had."

We sit there quietly for a long time.

Ginny wants to march into the Bluebird Café right now and leave the children there but I don't want any more conflict or confrontations or dramatic situations so I get her to agree to wait until it is time to hand the children over in the parking lot.

By the time Mrs. Gourd arrives I am angry too. Nellie, Madame Crenshaw, Mrs. Gourd, that bogus channeler with her great destinies and evolved people. My own stupidity at ever believing any of them. I will believe in no one ever again. What was the purple circle of light? Mrs. McCarthy? Coincidence? Wanting to believe? I will believe in nothing, then.

"We know what really happened," says Ginny, holding the baby carrier tightly so Mrs. Gourd can't get away. "Dr. Callahan told us that *you* dropped a stethoscope on Willie Mae's head."

"He's wrong," says Mrs. Gourd quickly.

"Well, shall we all go over and ask him?" asks Ginny.

I don't think I could talk to a grown-up like this but Ginny is in some ways already grown up.

"What if I did? More fools you," says Mrs. Gourd, grabbing at the baby carrier. "Anyhow, you can't prove nothing."

"Well, here's your perfectly fine baby back," says Ginny, handing over Willie Mae. "Nobody's going to babysit for you anymore."

"Like I can't figure that one out," says Mrs. Gourd, and walks away. No apology. Nothing.

Ginny and I stand in the parking lot and watch them until they disappear. We sit on a cement divider. Gulls swoop in a lavender light as the sun relaxes into the dinner hour. Ginny finally gets up and says she'd better go home and I sit for a few minutes longer when Ned's car pulls into the parking lot.

"NED!" I say in surprise.

"Fancy meeting you here, Bibles!" says Ned, unloading groceries.

"Never call me that again," I say.

"Come on, help me carry this stuff. I would have called your mother but—"

"No phone," I say.

"We're having a real blowout tonight. Champagne. Two kinds of pop. Lamb chops! Because *I* got a job."

When we get to the house he tells us the whole story. My mother is astonished. But it turns out the job isn't here in town or even in Massachusetts. The job is in Saskatchewan teaching French. It's a good full-time position, the type of job Ned has never held before, and he has even bought a house. He says the town needs a French teacher so badly that it is willing to assume the mortgage until Ned can pay back the down payment.

"It's a honey of a house," he says. "Of course, it's not very big. It's just kind of a box. Not a lot of personality. But it has three bedrooms. The town's got a lot of empty houses—that's why the school board got it so cheap. I have some snapshots in the car. I'll go get them."

He heads back to the parking lot. Maya and Max and Hershel go with him. They are all feeding potato chips to the gulls as they head down the beach.

My mother begins to get dinner ready. I am wondering if Ned actually thinks my mother would ever leave this house and move to Saskatchewan and I am thinking that I feel sorry for him and the disappointment he will have. Suddenly there is a tug on my neck and I am choking. I am too startled to cry out and then I smell something foul as a strong hairy arm pulls me backward. For some reason it is all this coarse, curly hair that scares me the most. There is something wrong about all this coarse, smelly hair. I cannot call out. I cannot move. I can't even register exactly what is happening. I blink rapidly. I see my mother coming out of the house, her eyes enormous, running to me, and I want to go to her but the arm tightens and a voice drawls, "Hold it right there, Mizz Fielding, it is Mizzzzz Fielding, isn't it?"

I know what the matter is now. The man is drunk. He is saying "Mizzzzz," like a buzzing bee. It sends chills down my arms.

He pulls me by the neck across the sand so that my heels drag. It hurts and I am afraid of choking to death and I can see by my mother's wide eyes that she is afraid of this too. She stops in her tracks and one hand goes to her throat as if she can feel mine. "I'm takin' her home to babysit, Mizzzz Fielding."

Then I know who it is. It is Mr. Gourd. I have

never heard him so drunk but I remember the day we heard him throwing things in the trailer. He is staggering left and right and sometimes it feels as if he isn't aware of me even though he has a fore-arm pressed so tightly against my neck.

"Taking her home?" repeats my mother in a croaking whisper. Then more loudly, "Why, you're the janitor at the school, aren't you? Please. Please stay calm."

"I *am* calm," he says, and laughs and staggers again. Every time he staggers he tightens his arm as if holding on to me for support and I can't get my breath for a minute. I hear strange animal sounds and realize they are coming from me. I see my mother's eyes get even larger as we listen to me.

"Yeah, I gotta take her home. Mrs. Gourd says she had to quit her job because this one doesn't babysit for us no more but I said, Don't worry, I'll get her. I got her now. She kin baysit." He stops and with a free hand removes a bottle from his pocket and takes a swig. "We gonna pack up and move now to 'nother town. Haul her with us to baysit. She almost killed the baby. You hear that? Dropped something on his head. Bible."

I think my mother is going to faint. She is sway-
ing. Instead, she says calmly and clearly, "Don't
worry, Mr. Gourd. I will never CALL 911! I will
never CALL 911!"

I think this is such an odd thing to say. It is part
of this nightmare of things suddenly off-kilter.
Why is she saying this?

"Don't you call NO ONE!" he yells savagely in
my ear. He totters a bit and then starts dragging
me again. I can't breathe and my mother starts running toward us but stops when he holds the hand
with the whiskey bottle out to the side threaten-
ingly as if he will strike me.

My mother is twisting her hands but she isn't
looking at him or me. She is looking behind us and
she seems even more terrified by what she sees
there and I am thinking, What can be worse than
this? when suddenly I am yanked backward and
then I fall in the sand away from Mr. Gourd. I seem
to bounce to my feet and start running without
thought, before I realize that Ned must have pulled
Mr. Gourd off me. But when I turn I see it is Mrs.
Spinnaker, sitting on the small of Mr. Gourd's back,
her legs still around his middle. She is so small she

must have *jumped* on him. She has his head pushed into the sand. My mother is sitting on him as well. The whiskey bottle is next to him. Then we hear a siren.

"I heard you yelling 'Call 911! Call 911!' I looked out the window and I called the sheriff," says Mrs. Spinnaker. "And then I thought, What can I do? What can I do? That man is drunk as a skunk and Jane is going to get hurt and I see I can creep around the side of the house and leap on his back before he hears me coming."

The sheriff arrives now, running, and takes control so my mother and Mrs. Spinnaker move off to the side, away from Mr. Gourd, who is in handcuffs.

"Oh, Mrs. Spinnaker, Mrs. Spinnaker! You were so brave!" says my mother. "How can I ever, ever thank you enough? You saved Jane's life. You saved her *life!*"

"And you saved Horace's. So we're even," says Mrs. Spinnaker, looking pleased at the praise.

"No, no, it's not the same *at all*. I can never, ever repay *you*," says my mother.

"Oh, so *that's* what you think of Horace!" says

Mrs. Spinnaker, her face darkening. "I might have known." And she storms back to her cottage in a huff.

My mother watches her go in dismay and looks like she would like to go after her but then says, "Enough, enough for one day, enough, enough."

And then I very quietly faint.

············

When I wake up the sheriff is leading Mr. Gourd away. He offers to take me to the hospital but I do not want to go and all I have are a few scratches on my neck where Mr. Gourd's fingernails raked me when Mrs. Spinnaker jumped on his back and he tried to hang on to me. My mother has gotten out the Band-Aids and antibiotic ointment. She cleans me up but we don't even talk, we are so stunned.

Ned has returned and is feeding and putting Max and Maya and Hershel to bed.

My mother and I cannot eat. We take a slow walk on the beach. She has not asked me once about any of it although the cat is out of the bag about dropping the Bible and all that followed.

Because Mr. Gourd has already mentioned it, I tell her about Willie Mae and Mrs. Gourd and the dropped Bible. So that she will know that Mrs. Gourd lied. That I did not drop a Bible on Willie Mae. Still, it is only a lucky accident that I didn't seriously hurt someone. What will she think of me that at one point I thought I had, and kept this secret all summer?

Our legs grow tired. The sun is soft and full and golden as it dips in a haze toward the sea. We finally return to the porch.

My mother and I sit quietly on the steps with our sides touching. Our legs are bent and we lean over our knees. I can hear her breathing along with the waves. "We all belong here equally, Jane," she says. "Just by being born onto the earth we are accepted and the earth supports us. We don't have to be especially good. We don't have to accomplish anything. We don't even have to be healthy."

I put my hands over my eyes and press the flesh back in hard. In relief it is melting off my bones. We sit there all through the twilight. I lean into my mother's side and cry.

To Canada

My Fourteenth Adventure

The last two weeks of summer are a blur. Ned and my mother get married quietly at the town hall without telling anyone until it is done. Mr. Gourd takes a plea and does not have to go to trial. My mother finishes making the rest of the blackberry jam until she has filled the last shelf. This is somehow satisfactory even though she has said that we cannot take it with us. She doesn't want to take all that jam over the border and besides, there is no room in Ned's car. He has traded his old car for a station wagon but even so, with all of us and our clothes and a few things it is full. My mother explains that we will all come back to the house for the summer and maybe if it doesn't work out in Saskatchewan Ned can try to find a job here.

"But we will never sell the house?" I ask.

"We will never sell the house," says my mother with one hand on a doorjamb as if she is reassuring it as well.

"Still, all that jam," I say sadly.

"I have an idea about that," she says.

Mr. Gourd has gone to jail and we go to visit Mrs. Gourd. She is angry with us. She thinks somehow it is all our fault.

"I had to quit my job," she says to my mother after we knock on the door of the trailer. "You probably heard that. And now without Dennis's salary we're going to have to give up the trailer too. Just where do you think me and my babies are going to live? I can't work. I got no one to watch them so I can't get a job. I got no money, no husband, no home."

"You can live in our house," says my mother.

Mrs. Gourd just stands there, her eyes doing their mechanical brain movement, back and forth and this way and that. Finally it seems to register.

"What about you?"

"We're going to Saskatchewan," says my mother. "You can live in our house until next summer when we return. As you can see, it's only a stopgap solution but maybe it will see you through to better times."

"That's very kind of you," says Mrs. Gourd. She spits it out like she can't quite believe it herself. I don't think she knows any other way to talk but grumpy.

"I still can't work. I got no one to watch my kids."

I know a solution suddenly but I don't want to say it. I tell her about Mr. Fordyce despite myself. My mother looks surprised when I mention him but says nothing.

"Well, I can't pay him much," says Mrs. Gourd.

"He'll probably do it for free. I think he likes children," I say. "I think he wants a job and someone to read to."

"You tell him I can't pay him," says Mrs. Gourd quickly.

I tell her where his trailer is and we leave her heading over there with the children to talk to him.

"I hope she likes the house," says my mother.

"Are you *nuts*?" I say. "She'd just better hope *you* like the prairies!"

254 ---- my one hundred adventures

"Oh, I do," says my mother.

Then she tells me about the road trip that she and Ned took in a falling-apart car when they were "young and wild."

"You were in love with Mr. Fordyce and H.K. and the clothes hanger man, back then, weren't you?"

"Well, yes, I guess in a way, but I *really* loved Ned and when he came back I loved him all over again. On this car trip we took, we stayed one night on the prairies. It is so beautiful in the grasslands. You can see the wind before you hear it, moving the long grasses. You can see the weather before you feel it. We stayed with some of Ned's friends in a farmhouse they owned in the middle of nowhere. You could look out of any window and see nothing but flat ground to the horizon. Imagine. I was helping Freda, his friend, make pies with cherries she had picked from her own tree. We were rolling out the dough and you could feel the barometric pressure drop. She looked out the window. It made her nervous. There was a quiet excitement in the air. Even the birds stopped and the horizon grew black and lightning flashed from up high in the sky all the way to the ground. The men were out scurrying to bring in the horses. Freda kept watching for funnels coming down from the clouds. They'd had tornadoes before. And everyone was worried but I was rolling out pie dough, so contented, so peaceful, so stilled with everything else, waiting for the storm."

My mother's face is alight with the memory and I realize that I don't need to worry about her leaving this place. To her all places are this place.

"Those kids better not pee on any of our beds," I say.

"We'll put rubber sheets on them before we leave," says my mother.

"We'll put rubber sheets on *everything*," I say.

············

The next day Ned and I walk into town to buy rubber sheets.

"I thought you didn't like having a stationary job and being settled," I say as we walk slowly through the sand, no hurry to do anything today, we're really just waiting to leave for Saskatchewan.

"Well, with that poet sniffing around your mother I knew I'd have to do something or I didn't stand a chance. I had to have something to offer her. That's why I went back to Canada. To see what I could scrounge up in terms of a stable job. Oh, say!" He reaches into his jeans pocket and pulls out some snapshots and hands them to me. "I got these from the car the other day and in all the excitement forgot to show them to you. There's the house, and that's what the countryside looks like. I know it looks kind of empty with nothing much to see."

It is endless waves of land with nothing on it. It *is* bleak and barren and empty with nothing much to see. But where have I heard these words before? Then I remember and gasp.

"Well," says Ned sheepishly, "it's not so bad as *that*. I grant you your first views of Saskatchewan are like, Who the heck would live there? But between the broiling-hot summers and the freezing-cold winters, the tornadoes and flies, why, it's practically a paradise."

"It's not that," I say. It is Madame Crenshaw's words coming back. How soon I was to go "someplace empty with nothing much to see." I had

stopped believing in mystic happenings and miracles. I had thought Madame Crenshaw nothing
but a con artist and a thief. Not a visionary. But it
appears she can be both.

"What's the matter with you?" he asks.

"I'm just trying to figure something out," I say. I
cannot tell him about Madame Crenshaw. I look at
him and wonder if he is my father. If I want to
know whose father Ned is or if he's anyone's, now
is the time to ask. But the moment passes and with
it my nerve. I cannot ask him any more than I can
tell my mother all my adventures any more.

Is this what it is to get older, to have adventures
you can no longer tell your family because you are
moving apart from them? Is this why my mother
likes to have Ned around, so that she has someone
to whom she can always tell her adventures? Or do
you grow up and have adventures you tell no one?
Are some adventures only yours alone? Will my
mother have adventures she won't even tell Ned?

"Figure out what?" Ned asks as he turns to look
down at me, maybe because I have been staring
at him.

"I am thinking that if I count my adventures this

summer, there weren't one hundred and I am wondering when the rest will come. Or if they will. I want my life to be a series of adventures. I want a hundred."

"Bibles, you're going to *CANADA*. You're going to have nothing *BUT* adventures."

············

The last few days of summer I spend on the beach. We build fires at night and Ned shows us how to find the North Star by looking first for the Big Dipper. I cannot go out at night now without seeing the Big Dipper and it feels to me as if it is looking at me, aware of me too. There is the sound of Canada geese in the mornings, honking and flying south, as we will be going north. We are just changing places. The Big Dipper will find us all in new locations. We are not moving so far from its perspective, perhaps.

Maya and I have started a lucrative restaurant with a menu of minnows and sand pies and crayfish. Her paper dolls come to order meals there. Sometimes Hershel does too. We have had to tell him twice not to eat the things we serve. Max does not see whales anymore. I see summer's curtain closing and behind it something closing for him as well. More often than not, when my mother sits on the porch steps now, we are totally silent. I think we are memorizing the sound of the waves.

Saying goodbye to Ginny is the worst. I go over to her house the night before we leave, but she solves the problem by telling her mother she won't see me. She will write to me in Saskatchewan. "I don't say goodbye," says the note she has left her mother to pass on to me, and I think of Ginny with her breaking heart, and leaving her alone now with all that drive and desire, and I figure that will give me something to worry about all the way to Saskatchewan.

On the way home through town I see Nellie stumping along with groceries and I call out, "Nellie! Madame Crenshaw was right! About going someplace barren? I'm going to Saskatchewan." She stops and gives me a long look and then trots on, busy and driven as Ginny, with her dreams and obsessions.

The next day Mrs. Gourd and her children come

over. My mother shows her the jars of jam. She
tells her that next summer she will teach her how
to make her own. Mrs. Gourd says she can't afford
all the berries but my mother takes her for a walk.
She shows her the blueberry bogs and the clam
beds and the places where the wild orach grows.

about the author

Polly Horvath is the highly acclaimed author of many books, including the National Book Award winner *The Canning Season*, the National Book Award nominee *The Trolls*, and the Newbery Honor Book *Everything on a Waffle*. *Publishers Weekly* has described her writing as "unruly, unpredictable, and utterly compelling," adding that "Horvath's descriptive powers are singular . . . her uncensored Mad Hatter wit simply delicious, her storytelling skills consummate."

Polly Horvath lives in Metchosin, British Columbia.